THE PERSIAN
ASSASSIN

A JUDGE MARCUS FLAVIUS SEVERUS
MYSTERY IN ANCIENT ROME

ALAN SCRIBNER

Torcular Press

Also by Alan Scribner

Marcus Flavius Severus Mysteries in Ancient Rome
Mars the Avenger
The Cyclops Case
Marcus Aurelius Betrayed
The Return of Spartacus
Mission to Athens
Across the River Styx

Anni Ultimi: A Roman Stoic Guide to Retirement, Old Age and Death
Co-authored by J.C. Douglas Marshall

ISBN: 9781688453586 (paperback)

Library of Congress Control Number: 2019913200
Amazon Kindle Direct Publishing
Seattle, Washington

Dedication
Ruth and Paul

TABLE OF CONTENTS

Personae xi

   Ancient Rome xv

   Map of the vicinity of Rome.............................xvi

SCROLL I 1

I	Marcus Flavius Severus: To Himself 3
II	Emeritus..5
III	A letter from the Emperor 9
IV	A visit from the *curiosi* 17
V	Posidippus, Lucius Verus' doctor.........29

SCROLL II...35

VI	A conference is held............................37
VII	Jangi, the Persian translator 47
VIII	An assassination attempt.....................53

IX   The *cubicularius* Eclectus, a cleaning
            slave and the Praetorian Lothar are
            questioned 59

X   Severus and Artemisia talk to
            Plautilla, a former Vestal Virgin 65

XI   A letter to the Emperor 75

SCROLL III 77

XII   Hunting for an Egyptian cobra 79

XIII   Straton travels to the Marsic cult
            and makes a discovery 87

XIV   Severus questions the *munerarius*
            and his slave 95

XV   Severus visits a *Mithraeum* 105

XVI   What Publius Pudens said 115

XVII   What Nush said 121

SCROLL IV 129

XVIII   Pre-trial preparations 131

XIX   The treason trial 143

XX   Severus Returns to Lanuvium and
            once again questions suspects 149

XXI   Severus asks the slaves of the villa
            for help 163

XXII   A letter from Plautilla 167

SCROLL V 175

XXIII   Dendron 177

XXIV   In the courtroom for judicial
torture 189

XXV   Straton meets Pectillus at a
bookstore 197

XXVI   The *curiosi* report on the suspects
at Lanuvium 201

SCROLL VI 203

XXVII   Vulso returns from Antium with
the will of Pudens 205

XXVIII   Judge Severus exposes the Persian
assassin 209

EPILOGUE
Marcus Flavius Severus: To Himself 221

Historical Note 227

PERSONAE

Judge Severus' familia and court staff
Marcus Flavius Severus – judge in the Court of the Urban Prefect and *iudex selectus*
Artemisia – Severus' wife
Aulus, Flavia, and Quintus, their 18, 16 and 10-year old children
Alexander – Severus' freedman and private secretary
Quintus Proculus – court clerk
Gaius Sempronius Flaccus – judicial assessor
Caius Vulso – centurion in the Urban Cohort
Publius Aelianus Straton – *tessararius* in the Urban Cohort
Argos – family dog
Phaon – family cat

Brennus – agent of the *curiosi*
Posidippus – doctor
Lucius Verianus Diogenes Jangi – Persian translator
Eclectus – *cubicularius*
Lucius Verianus Lothar – Praetorian cavalryman
Plautilla – former Vestal Virgin

Epaphroditus – *vilicus*, head of the Imperial villa at Lanuvium
Cynthia, Lysandra – slaves at the Imperial villa

Lucius Sergius Paullus – Prefect of the City of Rome
Lucius Claudius Anxius – assistant curator of the Imperial zoological collection
Decimus Dentatus – private collector of animals
Pectillus – slave of the Urban Cohort
Paternus – high priest of the Marsic cult
Teucer – priest of the Marsic cult

Gaius Obesus – *munerarius* at the Flavian amphitheater
Nush – Obesus' slave
Publius Plautius Pudens – Roman of Senatorial Class, devotee of Mithra
Claudius Cassius Casca – lawyer for Pudens
Dendron – Pudens' private secretary
P. Coellius Apollonaris – Roman Consul

The story is set in Rome and Lanuvium, 19 miles south of Rome, in the summer of the year 169 CE, 9 months after the events in *Across the River Styx*.

Roman hours: The day was divided into 12 day hours, starting from sunrise and 12 night hours from sunset. The length of the hour and the onset time of the hour depended on the season since there is more daylight in summer, more night in winter. In the spring and fall, close to an equinox, the hours were approximately equal to ours in length, with the 1st hour of the day at 6-7 am and the 1st night hour at 6-7 pm. The events in this book take place in the summer. A day hour can last up to an hour and 15 minutes, while a night hour is correspondingly shorter, 45 minutes. For simplicity, the equinox times of the hours mentioned in this book are:

1st hour of the day – 6-7 am
2nd hour of the day – 7-8 am
3rd hour of the day – 8-9 am
4th hour of the day – 9-10 am
5th hour of the day – 10-11 am
9th hour of the day – 2-3 pm
10th hour of the day – 3-4 pm
11th hour of the day – 4-5 pm
1st hour of the night – 6-7 pm
2nd hour of the night – 7-8 pm
3rd hour of the night – 8-9 pm
9th hour of the night – 2-3 am

Ancient Rome

The picture on the left shows the model of ancient Rome in the Museum of Roman Civilization in Rome.

The numbers on the picture locate places mentioned in the book, according to the following key.

1. Forum of Augustus, where Judge Severus has his courtroom and chambers
2. Praefectura building
3. Castra Praetoria
4. Aventine Hill *domus* of Publius Pudens
5. Caelian Hill *insula* of Judge Severus

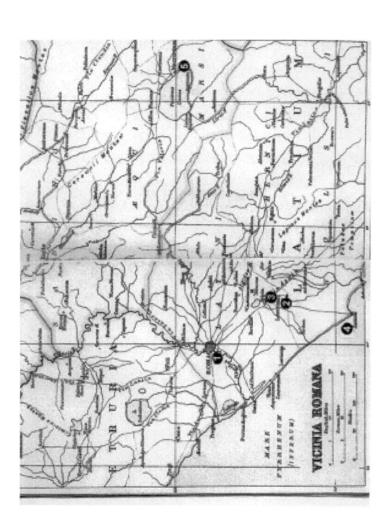

Map of the vicinity of Rome

The numbers on the map locate places in the vicinity of Rome mentioned in the book, according to the following key.

1. Rome
2. Lanuvium and the Imperial villa
3. Lake Nemi and the Severus retirement villa
4. Antium
5. Marruvium on Lake Fucinus and the Marsi cult

SCROLL I

I

MARCUS FLAVIUS SEVERUS: TO HIMSELF

"The Fates lead the willing; the unwilling they drag." So says Seneca. While I don't believe in the Fates literally, just as I don't believe in the gods except as mythology, sometimes their stories are apt, sometimes there is wisdom.

Take the case of the Persian assassin. There I was happily and willingly retired from public service to pursue my interests in astronomy and history, in reading and relaxing, in thinking and contemplation, in spending time with my family, when I was dragged back into tracking down a criminal. This time the crimes were espionage and assassination. This time I was up against an agent of the *spasaka*, the 'eye' of the *shahanshah*, the king of kings, the Great King of Persia, or Parthia as the current ruling dynasty of Iran is called. This time the assassin's targets were our Emperors, Marcus Aurelius and Lucius Verus. The reason was revenge. Revenge not just because they commanded the counterattack that defeated the Persian invasion of our Empire, but revenge because our legions had unjustifiably sacked their capital of Ctesiphon. This was what was feared and believed by our own secret service in espionage –the *curiosi*. And this fear had substance because Lucius Verus died at the age of 39 in January of this year, a few months ago, of what the doctors called *apoplexia*. He had suffered a stroke while in a carriage travelling back to Rome from the German front. It left him unable to move or talk for 3 days and then he died.

But what brought on the stroke? Was it natural? Or had someone poisoned Verus? If someone had, had it been an agent of the *spasaka*? For this is what our spy in Persia had led the *curiosi* to believe.

And so the Fates in the form of a request from Marcus Aurelius dragged me into the case of the Persian assassin. I could not refuse. After all, the Emperor was my friend from childhood and his life was threatened.

Or was it? Was this a real threat? Or was it a case of fear gone rampant? Was I chasing an assassin or a chimera? It was my fate to be dragged into finding out.

II

EMERITUS

Judge Severus appeared at the Praefectura building at the 3rd hour of the morning on the *Nones* of April. He had come there to meet with the new Urban Prefect, Lucius Sergius Paullus. Paullus was a senator and had been Consul the year before. And before that he had been Proconsul of Asia, the province where he had been born. Now he was chosen to replace the previous Urban Prefect, Quintus Junius Rusticus. Severus had worked with Rusticus for years, but he didn't know Paullus at all.

Both men were dressed in formal dazzling white togas. The Prefect's was arranged to show the broad red-purple stripe of the Senatorial Order on the tunic under his toga. Severus' toga was arranged to display the narrow red-purple stripe of the Equestrian Order on his tunic.

"*Salve*" – be well – began the Prefect, exchanging greeting kisses on the lips with Severus in the Roman style for family, friends and peers. For the rest a kiss on the cheek or a handshake would do.

"I'm very glad to meet you."

"*Salve*" replied Severus, in return, "I am very glad to meet you as well."

Both men were about the same height, taller than average. The Prefect was noticeably fatter than Severus, whose frequent workouts with the javelin kept him in good shape. The Prefect's face was etched with experience and he exuded strength. Severus' piercing gray eyes, slightly hawkish nose and intelligent look made his appearance every bit as formidable as the Prefect's.

Severus was shown to a comfortable chair across a table from where the Prefect sat down. The table was set with elegant transparent glasses already filled with white wine and a bowl of fruit. Severus took a sip of wine.

"Falernian," said the Prefect, unnecessarily, as Severus recognized the vintage from years of drinking the famous wine from the slopes of Mount Falernus.

The Prefect also took a sip of wine from his glass and bit into a fig. "I look forward to working with you, Severus. I know your reputation for solving difficult cases and the Emperor tells me you are a personal friend, not only now, but from childhood."

"Yes. Marcus Aurelius and I grew up together in the same neighborhood on the Caelian Hill. We played ball games together in the streets. I got to know him again a few years ago when he made me a special judge to investigate a case in Alexandria. We've been friends again ever since, though the all-consuming duties of a dutiful Emperor and his presence on the German frontier have made our meetings few and far between."

"Very interesting, Severus. Perhaps sometime you will tell me what our Emperor was like as a child. But for now, your message requested a meeting with me. Was it simply to get to know each other? Or did you have another purpose in mind?"

Severus took a deep breath and spent a moment clearing his mind and feeling comfortable.

"I want to remove my name from the panel of judges because I am retiring. As Seneca once put it, one's last years should be spent not on the turbulent sea of career and public affairs, but in port, in quietude, pursuing wisdom. 'Withdraw your worn neck from the yoke', he said. So that's what I am going to do. I wish to retire, to become *emeritus*."

The Prefect looked a little perplexed. "May I ask how old you are? You don't seem that old. Are you ill?"

"No. And contemplating retirement, I have perhaps never been healthier."

"But you are not that old."

"I am 48. Old enough. Particularly when I contemplate the shortness of life. The co-Emperor Lucius Verus died only a few months ago from a heart attack and he was only 39 years old."

"But lots of people live long lives, many even into their 80's, 90's and even beyond 100. We know that from the census."

"Yes. I know that is true and a few years ago I was told that according to the actuarial statistics compiled by the Bureau of the Treasury for tax predictions, anyone reaching my age should live at least until his 60s. Nevertheless, that is all irrelevant. Now I want to devote my time to liberal studies, to history and astronomy, to reading, to my family, to contemplation. I'm tired, even fed up, with enforcing the criminal laws in Rome. I don't want to deal any more with venality and evil. I want to lead a different life. I want to retire. I know I can continue in the courts, but 'the die is cast'."

"I suppose there is nothing I can do or say that will change your mind?"

"No. There isn't."

"Then I can only wish you good fortune and to tell you that I will miss your help in governing the City."

With that, and after a few polite pleasantries, Severus left, went home to his luxury apartment on the Caelian Hill, threw off his toga and embraced his wife.

Artemisia looked at him and saw that his face was glowing. She thought he had hardly looked more handsome. She returned a broad smile and Severus thought she had hardly looked more beautiful. Freedom encloaked them and they hugged each other closely and warmly.

"Is everything ready?" asked Severus after a while.

"Everything is packed and ready to go. We have one *carpentum* coach for us and the children, one for the slaves and two more for the possessions we're taking."

"The die is cast," replied Severus. "Let's go."

And they did, at dawn the next morning.

III

A LETTER FROM THE EMPEROR

The first month of retirement was glorious.
Their villa was located in the Alban hills
southeast of Rome, off the 18th milestone on the Via
Appia, and close to Lake Nemi, a circular lake in a
volcanic crater.

It took a good day's travel, including rest stops, to
reach it from Rome by *carpentum* coach. The Via Appia
was an excellent paved highway, with its large paving
stones and cement interstices formed into a smooth
surface all the way from the City and beyond. On flat
parts one might make 4 or 5 miles an hour. But there
were steep gradients in the hills and the side road from
the Appian way to the villa was further uphill and more
rustic. Still, the views were panoramic, breathtaking
and inspiring. The lake was cool and inviting. The air
was country air – clear, crisp and bracing, a huge difference from the smoggy *aer infamis* of the City.

The villa was small but elegant, with a white
6-column colonnade at the entrance, a garden and

a swimming pool behind. In the garden there was a beautiful plane tree, whose flat top not only provided shade on a hot summer's day, but recalled to Severus and Artemisia the original Academy of Plato at Athens, where Plato was wont to hold intellectual discussions outside under a shady plane tree.

Inside there was the usual atrium and peristyle and rooms for the children and the slaves. The walls were tastefully frescoed with geometric designs in the atrium and peristyle and scenes from nature in the bedrooms and *triclinium* dining room. There was also a library room where a nice portion of the family's 1,000 volume home library had been installed in cubbyhole shelving. What books to take and what to leave in the City apartment was one of the most difficult decisions of the move, provoking endless discussions, always inadequate. For whatever was left behind in Rome somehow turned out to be just the book one felt like consulting or reading the next day at the villa. Still, Severus had chosen volumes of history and astronomy for study in retirement, while Artemisia had brought research material for the new book she was working on, a biography of Aspasia, the famous partner of Pericles of Athens 600 years before. The children had also selected books for their own interests. 16-year old Flavia brought poetry and literature, 10-year old Quintus, a precocious child, books on mathematics and geometry. Alexander brought books on philosophy and general knowledge, especially Pliny the Elder's entire encyclopedic work on everything. The oldest son, 18-year old Aulus, was not with them. He was on his way to take up a post on the staff of a Tribune of the Legion XII Fulminata in the East.

The dream of retirement was fostered on the first night. Well after everyone was asleep, at about midnight, Artemisia gently prodded her husband and asked whether he was up. "I am now," he replied sleepily but with a certain eagerness in his voice. They had prearranged what was to come.

Both got up wearing only their light sleeping tunics, held each other's hands and silently left the villa, heading down a path to the lake a short walk away. Everything was silent except for some frogs and crickets and an occasional hoot from an owl. A bright half-moon provided illumination. Numerous stars ennobled a dark cloudless sky. When they reached the lake, they threw off their tunics and dove in. Refreshed, they swam back, lay down on the grass and embraced, making love in the cool night air under a cloudless sky of glittering stars and glowing moon.

Besides the attractions of the villa itself, its location on Lake Nemi was close to the Imperial villa at Lanuvium, only 3 miles away, less than an hour drive by *carpentum*. Though there were eight other Imperial retreats around Rome, the one at Lanuvium was the birthplace of the previous Emperor Antoninus and of Aurelius' young son Commodus, who was in line to become the next Emperor. And because Marcus Aurelius was vacationing there during this summer, his childhood friend Marcus Severus and his family were invited to visit every now and then.

In one visit, 10-year-old Quintus got to play with Commodus, 2 years younger than him, while 16-year-old Flavia got to know Annia Galeria, 2-years her senior. These were two of the Emperor's eleven children over the past 12 years, though four of them had already died before the age of 5. Commodus' twin, Titus, died at the age of 4 of an ear infection. The best doctors of the time could not save him.

As for the children Severus' children played with, Quintus reported to his parents that Commodus acted like a buffoon to suck up to him, singing and dancing at random. However, said Quintus, he could whistle better than anyone Quintus knew. "You should hear how he can whistle, Tata," exclaimed Quintus. "We may one day have a whistling Emperor. But otherwise all he's interested in is gladiators. And I'm interested in geometry and mathematics, so we didn't have much in common. I can't whistle at all."

Flavia had a much more agreeable friend in Galeria, both being interested in poetry and playing the cithara.

As for Severus and Artemisia, they had good times with Marcus Aurelius and his wife Faustina.

This reverie, this paradise, this fantasy, this idyll lasted for several months. But then one day, the *otium* of Severus, of Artemisia, of Quintus and Flavia, of Alexander, was interrupted while everyone was lying about the garden under the plane tree before lunch, discussing one of their favorite astronomy topics – the *via lactea*, the Milky Way in the night sky. What was it? Was it a band of milk spilled by the goddess Hera while feeding the baby Herakles, as Greek and Roman religion explained it? Or was it a merger of numerous distant stars too dim to discern individually, as many Natural Philosophers such as Democritus thought? In the Severus *familia*, the explanation of Democritus was totally embraced, the religious explanation ridiculed. But how could any explanation actually be proved? That was the problem they were grappling with.

But then Scorpus, the head slave of the household entered the garden and announced the arrival of a courier from the Imperial Post.

"Show him in," said Severus to Scorpus. "What could this be about?" he asked everyone else, a tone of annoyance, even trepidation, in his voice.

The courier entered and asked for Judge Severus and when Severus identified himself, gave him a scroll, announcing "A letter from the Emperor. I am to wait for a reply."

"Thank you," replied Severus. He turned to Scorpus. "Give him some refreshments while he waits."

Scopus escorted the courier into the villa while Severus unfurled the scroll and read:

"Marcus Aurelius Antoninus, Imperator, to Marcus Flavius Severus, greetings:

"I know, Marcus, that you have retired to a life of *otium* and liberal studies, just as Seneca advised and just as I would like to do someday. As you know, my desire is to be able to write history and from time to time I make notes about what I eventually want to incorporate into my book. This is all probably a hopeless dream on my part, yet I am pleased when a friend like you is able to achieve what I cannot.

"You will therefore realize that it grieves me to interrupt your retirement with a request I cannot avoid making. Marcus, our secret service, the *curiosi*, has told me that an assassin from Persia is on the loose in Rome. They believe he is out to kill me and that the death of my brother Lucius Verus a few months ago may have been an assassination. This may all be 'smoke' and nothing else. There may be no fire to produce it. Yet it cannot be ignored because one of our spies inside Persia has supplied information about the plot.

"The *curiosi* has been unable to find any assassin so far. But they have not given up the belief that an assassin exists. They say they need help and they even named you as the person they want to help them. They are aware, of course, of your reputation and ability to solve crimes. They remember in particular your brilliant solution of the murder of one of their agents and of General Cyclops a few years ago.

"I have therefore been importuned by the *curiosi* to give you a *cognitio* for this investigation. So while I regret interrupting your retirement to spend your time on this matter, I must ask you to help me out.

"If you agree, I will send a *curiosi* agent to brief you. He can be at your villa anytime convenient for you.

"*Vale*."

Severus let the scroll furl back up, let out a deep regretful sigh, and then unfurled it again and read it out loud to Artemisia and Alexander. When he finished he said, "I have no choice in the matter, do I? He is not just the Emperor, but my friend and he needs my help."

Both Artemisia and Alexander silently nodded in the affirmative. Alexander got up and went into the house to get a pen and scroll of his own and returned ready for Severus to dictate a reply.

"Marcus Flavius Severus to Marcus Aurelius Antoninus, Imperator, greetings:

"Any threat to your life must be stopped. I am totally at your service in this regard. To establish my authority and jurisdiction for this *cognitio*, I will need an appointment as *iudex selectus*, special judge, as I had for my cases in Alexandria and Athens. I will also need assigned to me to assist in this investigation, my previous staff, police aides from the Urban Cohort, Caius Vulso and Publius Straton, my law assessor, Gaius Flaccus, and my court clerk Quintus Proculus. The *curiosi* agent must come here as soon as possible to brief me on the case.

"You should have no qualms about interrupting my retirement. Your life unquestionably takes precedence.

"*Vale*."

The reply scroll was furled up, sealed and stamped with Severus' seal ring of a trireme and handed to the courier who left promptly.

"*Merda*," thought Severus to himself. "*Merda, merda, merda*."

Artemisia just shook her head in agreement and sympathy. She knew exactly what her husband was thinking.

IV

A VISIT FROM THE *CURIOSI*

Two mornings later, at the 5th hour, a *carpentum* 4-wheeled coach drew up in front of Severus' villa. It carried only one passenger, dressed in the plain white toga of a Roman citizen. To Scorpus who greeted the arrival of the vehicle, the passenger said only, "My name is Brennus. I am here to see Judge Severus."

Brennus was tall, with blonde hair, blue eyes, a Gallic name and a City of Rome accent. It was a good bet that his forebears were once slaves, captured in war perhaps. Now, as a high ranking *curiosi* agent, he was one of the most powerful men in Rome, if only behind the scenes.

Scorpus led him into the garden where Severus was slouched in a chair reading a book. He was dressed in a casual, dark blue tunic.

"*Eminentissime,*" the visitor addressed Severus using the honorific for a member of the Equestrian Order, "My name is Brennus, I am a member of the *curiosi*. The Emperor sent me."

Severus stood up and exchanged greeting kisses on the cheek.

"Please sit and feel free to take off that uncomfortable toga." Severus motioned to a chair on the other side of a garden table.

"Thank you." He removed the toga and handed it to Scorpus, who immediately left the two men alone. Under the toga Brennus wore an elegant white tunic with red geometric designs on the sleeves and hem. But there were no *clavi*, broad or narrow stripes signifying membership in one of the upper-class Orders. He was an ordinary citizen. This was normal for a *curiosi* agent, whose main task was internal security and the prying into subversive activities, particularly in the Equestrian and Senatorial Orders.

"Brennus? Aren't you the *curiosi* agent who worked with my police aide Caius Vulso some years ago in the case of General Cyclops?"

"One and the same, *eminentissime*. And I hope I will be able to work with him again on this case."

"You will. He is due to arrive here tomorrow."

Scorpus and another slave quietly entered the garden with a bowls of fruit and nuts, two glasses and carafes of wine and water. They silently put the refreshments on the table between the two men and silently and quickly withdrew. Severus motioned to Brennus to help himself, which he did, to wine.

"Tell me what you know," said Severus to the agent.

"Two months ago, a report from an agent of ours inside Iran reached Rome. The spy is a Persian who is in our pay. It is not only the Persians who have gold to spread around and buy intelligence. We do it as well. Anyway, our spy, let us call him Xerxes, though it is not his name, has given us important information in the past, particularly during the recent war with Parthia. Through him we occasionally had foreknowledge of Parthian military plans, which was very helpful to us. Now the war has been over for almost 5 years. We have sacked their capital city Ctesiphon and occupy Mesopotamia. Marcus Aurelius and co-Emperor Lucius Verus have even had a Triumph through Rome. But while that war may be over, there is always a rivalry and animosity between Rome and Persia, between West and East, that I don't believe will ever end. And for their part, there is a spirit for revenge, not only for the loss of the war, but especially for the sacking of their capital city, which they consider unnecessary and cruel.

"Now, it turns out that Xerxes not only has access to Parthian military secrets, but he sometimes has access to secrets of the *spasaka*, the 'Eye' of the Great King, which as you know is the Persian secret service. The *spasaka* is our counterpart, though it is much older than the *curiosi*,"

Severus helped himself to some of the wine and a few nuts and motioned to Brennus to help himself to more, which he did, to both wine and nuts. Then he continued.

"Two months ago, as I mentioned, we received a report from Xerxes. We don't know precisely when it was sent out because of the difficulties of communication and the length of time it takes to get a message from inside Persia to Rome. But months are usual for transmission time even during the sailing season. In winter, of course, it takes a lot longer.

"His report was astonishing. It said that the *spasaka* had hatched a plan to assassinate both Lucius Verus and Marcus Aurelius. They particularly wanted Lucius Verus killed because he was at the Persian front with our troops during the war and probably ordered the sacking of Ctesiphon."

"I thought though," interrupted Severus, "that Verus was only at the front once and for a short time, for show. The war was really run by our generals, Avidius Cassius and the others, while Verus dallied away his time with women and gambling and drinking. Didn't Panthea, supposedly the most beautiful woman in the world, become his mistress during that time?"

"Yes, that's true. She even got him to shave off his beard for her. But that's just a sidelight. Whether he was the real leader of our forces or not, he was certainly the titular leader, the face of the war for us and for the Parthians."

"And Lucius Verus is now dead."

"Yes, at the end of January, as everyone knows, he had a stroke, lingered for three days and then died. He was only 39 years old. Of course, we thought, as everyone did, that his death was the result of natural causes. It's not exactly unknown for healthy young men to die of strokes and Lucius Verus had a history of illness. But in view of the report from Xerxes, we now not only have to think about whether the death of Verus was really from natural causes or was he assassinated? And even more importantly, we have to guard against any assassination attempt against Marcus Aurelius. In other words, we have to take the report of our agent in Persia seriously. We have to regard it as true, unless proved otherwise."

"Do you have any corroboration or confirmation that the report is true? As you realize, it may be just smoke and nothing to worry about."

"We cannot determine which it is. It may be smoke. But it may not be. We are stymied. That's why we asked for your help."

"What have you done so far to investigate?"

"We are not sure what to do. But we started anyhow by grabbing three former slaves of Lucius Verus and torturing them to see what, if anything, they knew."

"And did anyone confess?"

"Yes. They all did. But all the confessions were false, as we found out. They confessed to stop the torture, that's all."

"Brilliant," said Severus with a visibly satirical sneer.

"I know, I know. I didn't order the torture. Our Princeps, the head of the *curiosi* did. He is a political appointee and doesn't know anything much about internal security work. He ordered torture to be able to say the *curiosi* is on the job. That's all. He said slaves are only 'speaking tools' anyway. So who cares?"

"I do."

Brennus made a rueful smile in return. "I do too. My own ancestors not that long ago were slaves from Gaul."

"What are you going to do next?"

"That's what I'm here to discuss with you and get your ideas about. What should we do next? There are a lot of possible roads to take. Emperors have huge entourages. Advisors, bureaucrats, friends, guards, freedmen, attendants, servants, slaves, hangers-on, sycophants, people seeking favors, you name it. Lucius Verus, for instance, had all these slaves and hangers-on who he brought back with him from the East – actors, cithara players, flute players, mimes, jugglers, women, sycophants, *et cetera*. We might have to question them one by one."

"It's none of them."

"How can you know that, judge?" said Brennus, surprised at Severus' statement. And a bit skeptical. "How can you say that?"

"Because if Xerxes' information is correct the assassin's assignment is to kill not just Lucius Verus but Marcus Aurelius as well, isn't that right?"

"Yes. So?"

"So the assassin must be someone able to gain access to both Verus *and* Marcus Aurelius. And these hangers-on of Lucius Verus, these actors and sycophants have no chance of becoming part of Aurelius' entourage. We have to look for someone who may have already become part of Aurelius' entourage in some way. That's where we should start. Do you know of anyone who was once part of Lucius Verus' court and is now part of Marcus Aurelius' or, if not a member of his entourage, has access to him?"

"I see what you mean. It's a good idea," replied Brennus, "A very good idea. It narrows our search to a few people for a start. We don't have to question everyone, to run this way and that like a chicken with its head cut off. I knew you were the right person to consult." He laughed. "I know you must be right because everyone has noticed that the friends of Lucius Verus all wore their hair long, like he did, while the friends of Marcus Aurelius wear their hair short, like him." Brennus began to think. Severus drank up his wine glass, poured himself another, and sipped it.

"There's the doctor, Posidippus. He treated Verus for three days after the stroke and is now part of Aurelius' entourage. Aurelius' personal doctor Galen has been home in Pergamum in Asia. Posidippus is one of his students and followers."

"What treatment did he give Verus, do you know?"

"He bled him. I know that."

"Bleeding often weakens patients and causes complications rather than healing, doesn't it?"

"So I've heard. But it is a standard treatment. It sometimes cures. I've heard that too."

"I want to see that doctor. Who else fits the profile? Access to both Emperors."

"There must be some members of the Praetorian Guard who were with Verus in the East and are now back in Rome guarding Marcus Aurelius. Maybe some of the Praetorian cavalry, the *equites singulares Augusti*, who personally stay close to the Emperor, may be who you're looking for.

"Find out if one of them was with Verus and is now with Aurelius. Who else?"

"I don't know off-hand. I'll find out and let you know within a few days. In the meantime, I'll send the doctor here to talk to you. I know he's in Rome because Marcus Aurelius is."

"Excellent. Then we have a place to start. The doctor. And here's another thought. Let's not overlook the obvious. Were there any Persians in Verus' entourage?"

"I think there was a translator. I don't know if he was Persian, though he might be. But I don't know where he is."

"Find him."

"I will."

Severus was silent for a few moments, thinking. "I think, Brennus, I will have to know more about our spy in Persia. Who is he? How does he come by the information? What precisely was it that he said about the assassination plot? Do you have it in writing? Or by word of mouth?"

"Usually our policy is to keep these things secret, very secret. Even I can't answer everything you ask."

"You have to change your policy in this case. In order to make a good assessment of the situation I have to know these things. I'll speak to the Emperor personally if the *curiosi* insists on being recalcitrant, and he'll order you to answer my questions, so you might as well save the time and trouble and tell me now."

Brennus was silent for a few moments, thinking.

"All right. Here's what I know. Our spy who for our purposes I'm calling Xerxes is a Persian. And he is a member of the *spasaka*. His information is therefore directly from the source."

"How did you succeed in placing a spy within the *spasaka*?"

"Actually, we didn't. Actually, he offered himself to us, offered to provide us with information. For a price. A lot of Roman gold was given to him. And he gave us good military and political information in return.

"This all was shortly after the Parthians invaded our territory, the year when Marcus Aurelius became Emperor. The accession of a philosopher-king seemed too good to miss for the Persians. So they tested him. Of course, we won the war. And Xerxes helped, I have to say.

"We don't know precisely when the message revealing the plot to assassinate our Emperors was first sent. It reached Rome two months ago by various means of communication. By letters, by fast couriers, by boat, by semaphore, by fire signals. All are used for the most rapid communication, but I don't know how Xerxes got his message to Antioch, for instance, which is where are eastern station is."

"You say fire signals might have been used. How does that work?"

The time for a signal must first be prearranged by the sender of a fire message and the receiver. Then the standard military signaling system is used. There are three torches, each of which encodes a third of the alphabet. One flash of the left torch means the letter A, two flashes B. The center torch encodes the next third of the alphabet and the right hand torch the last part. The flashes are produced by lowering the torch and raising it or by lowering and raising an opaque screen in front of the torch.

"The message is then passed from station to station by more fire signals, by semaphores, by couriers, by horse, by ship in the sailing season. The message goes first to Antioch in Syria where we have an eastern station, and then on to Rome. But as far as this message is concerned, we don't know when Xerxes first sent it or when he first learned of the plot, at the outset or sometime later. All we know for now is that it arrived in Rome two months ago from our station in Antioch. The fastest ship time is about 3 weeks in the summer, but winter is not the sailing season. So while it might have taken about a week to get from Persia to Antioch, though I'm guessing, I just don't know how long it took to get to Rome. The sailing season didn't start up again until Spring."

"What did the message that you received in Rome say precisely."

"It was quite simple. It said only 'Assassination of both emperors authorized.'"

"That's all? There's nothing, no hint about who the assassin might be? Or where or when he might strike?"

"No. Xerxes probably didn't know. Otherwise, I think he would have told us. But we have to act on what we know, don't we?"

"Yes. We have no choice."

Severus thought for a few moments. Then continued. "There is a caveat to this approach, however."

"What is that?"

"I remember at the time we were investigating the case of General Cyclops, you told my aide Vulso that the *spasaka* often bragged that they were responsible for the assassinations of both Philip of Macedon as he was on the brink of invading Persia and Gaius Julius Caesar as he was about to set out to conquer Persia."

"Yes. That is so. Although it may be just 'smoke'. After all, Caesar was assassinated by Romans –Brutus, Cassius and the others – while Philip was killed by one of his own bodyguards. There was no Persian involved."

"That's just the point I'm getting to. If the Persians had any involvement in those assassinations, it must have been by buying the assassins or otherwise spreading Persian gold in the right places to bring about the result. So if they use the same tactics here, it may be that our Persian assassin is the paymaster of the perpetrator. If that's the case, if the actual assassin is paid in Persian gold, then we should keep our eyes open for anyone who has access to Lucius Verus and Marcus Aurelius and who has recently become rich. He may have recently spent a lot of money on clothes, on women, on a house, on things of value."

"But he may not have flaunted his new found wealth."

"I know. But he may have. Keep our eyes open and make inquiries along these lines."

Brennus stood up. "This has been very fruitful."

"Will you stay to dinner?"

"I would like to. But now I have to get back to Rome as fast as I can and start the ball rolling. I'll have to find the doctor and send him here and also find out about the Persian translator."

Severus stood up as well and walked Brennus outside to his waiting *carpentum*. He then went back into the villa and called his private secretary.

"Alexander. What do you know about bleeding as a cure for a stroke?"

Alexander shrugged. "It's a standard treatment for anything, isn't it?

"See what you can find in our library about it. I'm going to question to the doctor who bled Lucius Verus. Maybe to save his life. Maybe to murder him."

V

POSIDIPPUS, LUCIUS VERUS' DOCTOR

"Bleeding," said Posidippus, the doctor who last treated Lucius Verus, "is not the first thing a doctor should do in treating a patient, unless the symptoms are serious, critical. Lucius Verus had a stroke and was paralyzed for three days. There was no indicated treatment except bleeding. That is the opinion of Galen and almost the entire medical profession except for the misguided school of Erisistratos who rejects bleeding and recommends starvation instead."

Posidippus was a gaunt man, with a sharp beak-like nose, sunken cheeks and long arms. The image of a vulture came to Severus' mind when he looked at him. But the doctor delivered his opinion about bloodletting forcefully and with some asperity at Severus for even questioning its use. And he delivered it in Greek in a superior tone of voice.

He downed a large gulp of wine from the cup on the table in the garden where they were sitting. Severus and Alexander, sitting opposite Posidippus, looked faintly horrified and amused at the doctor's condescending manner. Everyone knew that doctors, while necessary, were famously fallible. In their opinions and their treatments. They should be avoided, if possible.

"The cause of disease," the doctor went on lecturing, "is an imbalance in the humors of the body. There are four, as you should know. Blood, phlegm, black bile and yellow bile. If they are in harmony and balanced, a person is healthy. If not, there is illness, toxins having built up in the body. If a patient is very ill, he must be bled to get rid of the toxins, to restore the balance of the bodily humors. That's obvious, at least to the medical profession, if not to the layperson. The theory was developed by the great father of medicine Hippocrates and is still the best theory of disease and health, as the current teaching and writing of Galen make clear. Insightfully, he associates the four humors with the four elements and the four seasons. I can't go into the whole theory now, but I suggest you read Galen's recent book, *On the Elements According to Hippocrates.* It's true that Galen recommends diet as the most important treatment for most imbalances, but Verus had a stroke and was lying there paralyzed. Changing his diet was obviously not the indicated treatment, bloodletting was.'"

Alexander made a comment and asked a question. "I've looked over that book and note that Galen says that patients could die of bloodletting."

"Of course," countered Posidippus smoothly, "if you take too much blood. Bleeding must be carefully monitored by an expert to prevent adverse effects.

"In the case of Lucius Verus, he had a stroke and was paralyzed for three days. The only accepted treatment, almost a last resort except for surgery, is bloodletting, which I performed carefully. Indeed, a few years ago Verus was very ill and bloodletting cured him, so I was told.

"But let me ask you this, judge. Why all these questions? It's been about six months since Lucius Verus died. He died from natural causes after a stroke. Why are you asking about it now?"

"I'll explain. But first, do you know what caused the stroke?"

"I have no idea. *Apoplexia* happens all the time. Obviously the bodily humors become out of balance in those cases."

"Can strokes be induced?"

"Yes. By frightening some people too much, by poisoning, by too much pain, and other inducements to cause the sudden build-up of toxins."

"Can you tell if any of that happened in Verus' case?"

"Not unless I had witnessed the cause or been told about it. Usually it's all very natural and that's that. Are you suggesting Verus was murdered by inducing a stroke?"

"It's possible, isn't it?"

"Possible, perhaps. But as far as I know, that's not what happened."

"You say a stroke can be induced by poison, for instance."

"Yes. But I saw no sign of poison."

"Does poisons leave signs?"

"Some do. Like belladonna, for instance. It leaves a red splotch. I saw no red splotch."

"By the way, doctor. Did you like Lucius Verus?"

Posidippus' face took on a defiant, almost angry scowl. "It doesn't matter whether I liked him or not. I take the Hippocratic Oath, just like every doctor. I try to save lives, not end them, if that's what you're suggesting."

"But did you like him?"

"He was an Emperor. I am a mere doctor. It wasn't my place to like or dislike him. But from your question, I expect you've heard the false and vicious rumor that he seduced my wife, kept her for a week and then threw her out. I expect you've heard that that's why I bled him too much and deliberately killed him. Well, it's all false, just Roman *vituperatio*, just the invention of vicious slanderers. The gods ended his life, not I.

"And as for anyone trying to blame his death on me, you should be aware of the accusations these same slanderers voice against Marcus Aurelius. They say he murdered Verus by poisoning him. By putting poison on one side of a knife he cut meat with and giving the poisoned meat to Verus, while he ate the unpoisoned slice. Or was it oysters rather than pork, as another rumor has it. Or was it Verus' wife Lucilla, Marcus' daughter, who poisoned him in revenge for Verus sleeping with her mother. That's current gossip too, but really nothing but Roman *vituperatio*. And so are any accusations against me."

"There is this difference, however," shot back Severus. "I know for certain that Marcus Aurelius didn't poison Lucius Verus."

"How can you know that, may I ask?" replied the doctor with a slight sneer.

"Because I know the Emperor personally. I knew him as a child on the Caelian Hill where we both grew up, and I know him now as a friend. And I know that murder is not in his character. If he objects to someone, usually a look of silent disapproval will convey his censure. Or he can become pedagogical and at most lecture someone to death. But poisoning? Not possible for him. It's not in his character. And if there is one thing I've learned from my experience in the courts, character is the key to crime."

Posidippus made no reply.

"On a different topic, doctor, you are now a doctor to Aurelius, is that right?"

"Yes. His personal doctor Galen is away, back in his home in Pergamum, and I, as a student of Galen, was recommended by him and so have become a doctor to Aurelius, at least until Galen returns. Perhaps you know this about the Emperor, that he is something of a hypochondriac. One day it's his stomach, the next day his wrist, the next his leg, then a cold, then the stomach. There's always something. He and his rhetoric teacher Fronto write to each other almost daily, each complaining about their real or imaginary maladies. So Aurelius wants me nearby most of the time."

"Thank you doctor. You may go now, but I may call on you again."

Without a further word, the doctor got up, turned around and strutted away, his nose held high.

"What do you think, Alexander? Is he suspect?"

"He had the opportunity and the means. Those are arguments against him."

"Yes, they are, though, of course, they prove nothing. Even if he looks like a vulture."

Alexander laughed. "A vulture. Yes, that's what he looked like to me as well. So if I'm ever sick, make sure he's nowhere around. As we all know, vultures prefer their victims dead."

SCROLL II

VI

A CONFERENCE IS HELD

Three days later at the 2nd hour of the morning Judge Severus, accompanied by his wife Artemisia and his secretary Alexander, walked into his former chambers in the Forum of Augustus. His chambers were inside the Forum's elegant colonnade which surrounded the beautiful and splendid Temple of Mars the Avenger. The main venue for the public trials of the Court of the Urban Prefect was outside under the colonnade. When Severus arrived, Tribunals were being set up in the open for the public trials that occurred there on the 254 court days of the year.

The previous day they had driven into Rome by *carpentum* and stayed the previous night at Severus' apartment on the Caelian Hill. The children were still at the villa in the Alban hills, along with the household slaves. Early this morning, Severus, Artemisia and Alexander had walked down the Caelian hill to the Forum of Augustus. The weather would become hot as the summer day progressed, but it was not so

bad in the early morning. Nor had the air yet turned
into the *aer infamis*, the oppressive, smelly polluted
air that usually hovered over the City throughout the
day, especially in the summer. The fires and smoke of
morning cooking for a population of over a million
people combined with the industrial odors of smelt-
ing, of animal slaughtering, of myriad manufacturing
and business enterprises combined. They regularly
produced peculiar and horrific smells combatted only
by a welcome waft of wind or people holding personal
bags of flower petals to their noses.

When Severus retired, his chambers had been assigned to another judge, Gaius Memmius, who was
on the panel of judges for the Court of the Urban
Prefect. But when Severus received his new appointment as *iudex selectus* to delve into the Persian assassination plot, Judge Memmius had been ushered out
and Severus given back his chambers.

So while it was with some chagrin that Severus
had interrupted his retirement and returned to work,
it was with a lot more chagrin that Memmius had
been booted out of his new quarters. Still, when back
in his chambers Severus felt a surge of energy coming
from the prospect of action, of detection, of involvement. It did not entirely dispel his chagrin, but chal-
lenged it.

Quintus Proculus, the judge's court clerk, was
already in chambers and welcomed Severus back,
the two exchanging greeting kisses in the Roman
style. Proculus was old, no one knew how old except
Proculus himself, and he wasn't telling. And no one
cared because he knew the law and its procedures

better than most judges, lawyers and clerks, having spent a lifetime in the courts.

Severus surveyed his chambers and saw almost nothing had changed. The tall circular shelved wooden *scrinium* for scrolls and documents stood in the center of the room. An official painting of the Emperor Marcus Aurelius graced one wall and his desk and a long conference table and chairs were still in place. Only his elegant white reading couch was gone, replaced by a garish bright red and gold couch.

"Where's my couch?" Severus asked Proculus.

"Judge Memmius' wife removed it and took it to their apartment. She gave her husband this couch for his chambers since she liked yours better."

"Can I get my couch back?"

Proculus just shrugged. "I don't know. But I think you will have to use diplomacy of a high order. Memmius' wife seemed determined to have your couch for herself. And she's not someone I would want to tangle with. Behind her back people call her 'Medusa'."

Before Severus could even absorb the problem, his police aides, Caius Vulso and Publius Straton came into the chambers. They were on time. It was now the 3rd hour of the morning, when the court day usually started.

Greeting expressions of "*salve*" were exchanged all around, as were greeting kisses. Court slaves brought fruit and wine and set them on the conference table, while everyone took seats.

Caius Vulso was a centurion, a veteran of the legions, having served all over the Empire, from *Legio*

I Minervia on the border of Germania to *Legio* II
Traiana in Egypt. After 20 years, he took his retirement bonus instead of a land grant and came to Rome
to enlist in the Urban Cohort. Vulso was smart, self-
educated, sometimes brutal, but effective in getting
things done. He was not a man to mess around with
and Severus relied on his prowess.

"How is Aulus doing?" asked Vulso, referring to
Severus' 18-year-old son who had just joined the army.

"He received an appointment to the staff of a
Tribune with the legion XII Fulminata in Cappadocia,"
answered Severus.

"He should have arrived in the East by now,"
joined in Artemisia, "but we haven't heard from him
yet."

"He'll do fine," predicted Vulso. "Last I saw him
before he left, he was very serious about his new role
in life. Quite a change from the dissipated life he had
been leading at the gladiatorial games, in the brothels
and just hanging around."

"We also noticed the change," added Severus,
"and hope and believe he's almost a new person."

Publius Aelianus Straton was also a member of
the Urban Cohort, but his route to it was far different
than Vulso's. Straton had been a slave of the Imperial
household of the Emperor Hadrian as a child and
was manumitted at the Emperor's death. Thereafter
he wended his way through odd jobs in the city of
Rome until he got a fortuitous appointment to the
Urban Cohort, where he rose to the rank of *tesserar-
ius*, one rank below centurion. As a member of Judge
Severus' entourage, he became a valuable aide. With

his sad brown eyes and talent for passing unnoticed almost anywhere he had successfully played under-cover roles from street philosopher to wagon driver to religious enthusiast to just an ordinary street person.

As they were seating themselves at the table and helping themselves to the refreshments, Severus' for-mer assessor, Gaius Sempronius Flaccus, came in. More greeting kisses were exchanged all around.

Flaccus had been hired 11 years before as an asses-sor by Judge Severus straight out of the law school of Sabinus and Cassius, the same law school Severus had attended, as had his father and grandfather. Flaccus was smart, with a good sense of humor, and a rather off-hand casual attitude toward life. He had a good legal mind.

"I can only stay for about an hour," he told the judge as he took a seat. "I have to be in Judge Memmius' court at the 10th hour to argue a case."

"What kind of case?" asked Severus.

"An abortion case."

"Abortion? What kind of case is that? Abortions are not illegal. Is it a civil suit? Are you representing the plaintiff or defendant?"

"Abortions aren't illegal, of course, but the hus-band has a say in the matter. It's his child too, after all. If he agrees, no problem. If not, the woman can get an abortion, but it then becomes grounds for di-vorce, maybe even a fine. Anyway, I'm representing a woman who wants an abortion. The husband wants the child and has come into court arguing that the abortion shouldn't be allowed because, as Pythagoras says, the soul attaches to the fetus at the moment of fertilization. Therefore, the fetus with a soul is a person. The current legal and philosophic attitude, of course, is that the soul attaches only at birth so the fetus is not yet a person."

"There are other philosophic theories too, aren't there?" asked Artemisia. "Some say that the soul enters 40 days after fertilization for boys and 90 days for girls, though how anyone knows whether the fetus is a boy or a girl is beyond me."

"It's not beyond numerous people who claim they know," interjected Vulso. "Midwives, doctors, interpreters of dreams, charlatans. Many of them have an opinion, right or wrong."

"I know. They have a 50-50 chance of being right." She looked at her husband. "Remember your mother sent us an astrologer who kept on getting it wrong. We had a boy, then a girl, then a boy. The astrologer told us we would have a girl, then a boy, then a girl."

"Yes," continued Flaccus, "the whole issue is confused in many ways. Abortions are not illegal, but are looked down upon socially. It deprives the State of a citizen, for instance, as well as the family of an heir."

"But it's still the woman's choice, isn't it?" rejoined Artemisia.

"Yes. That's the current view of the law. The woman decides, but if the husband disagrees it can have consequences."

Before Flaccus could continue, the *curiosi* agent Brennus arrived and took a seat at the table while exchanging nods and smiles with Vulso whom he had worked with some years before in the case involving the murder of General Cyclops.

"Gaius," Severus turned to Flaccus, "we'll have to hear more about your case later." Then he addressed the assembled group. "Let me first bring you up to speed about this *cognitio* and what we've done so far."

Severus then reviewed the facts about the possible Persian assassin, about the possibility that the death of Lucius Verus was not a natural stroke, but a murder, and about how to prevent any attempt to kill Marcus Aurelius. He then reviewed his interview with Lucius Verus' doctor and the idea that possible suspects might be people who were in the entourage of Lucius Verus and managed after his death to enter the entourage of Marcus Aurelius. He mentioned the Persian translator for Lucius Verus and any member of the Praetorian guard who personally guarded Verus and now might be personally guarding Aurelius. Then he turned to Brennus. "Do you have any new information?"

The *curiosi* agent opened a cylindrical *capsa* carrying case with scrolls and waxed tablets inside, took out several and spread them out on the table in front of him. He began to unroll one of the scrolls.

"Do I have new information? Indeed, I do. First, regarding the Persian translator who was with Lucius Verus when he was at the front in the Parthian war. His name is Diogenes. He also has a Persian name, Jangi. He says he is a Roman citizen from Antioch in Syria. He's currently in Rome, having come here with Verus when he returned, and is now one of Marcus Aurelius' advisors about Persian affairs."

"I want to talk to him, of course," said Severus. "Where is he now?"

"He is living in an *insula* at the foot of the Palatine. And he's on the Palatine during the day, so I can have him here this afternoon if you'd like."

"Yes. Do that. I will question him this afternoon."

"Then there is the question of the Praetorian guard," continued Brennus. "There may be any number of praetorians who were with Verus in Persia and are now guarding Aurelius. I'm thinking especially of the cavalry wing of the Praetorians, the *equites singulares Augusti*, the horsemen who escort the Emperor when he travels. We don't know yet which ones accompanied Verus on campaign or which ones are with Aurelius now. But we will know in a day or two."

"Anything more?"

"Yes, in fact. Two other people to consider. The first is named Eclectus. He was a freedman and confidante of Verus and had the post of *cubicularius*. While Aurelius dismissed most of Verus' freedmen he took on one of them, Eclectus. Eclectus is now a *cubicularius* for Aurelius. A *cubicularius*, as you know, is a chamberlain, a master of the bedroom, a valet, often a confidante, often a member of the Emperor's *familia*, often an all-purpose factotum. I don't know yet how or where this Eclectus fits in, but I will find out."

"I want to talk to him too," said Severus.

"Of course. And then there's someone else. A curious possibility, perhaps. There's a woman named Plautilla, a former Vestal Virgin who has completed her 30-year stint of serving the goddess Vesta and is now free to marry, to have children, to live a normal life, to stop being a virgin. And from what I hear she has been pleasurably pursuing that endeavor since her release from the Temple of Vesta. Anyway, as you know, a former Vestal is one of the most desirable, influential and important women in Rome. Plautilla was therefore welcomed into Verus' entourage and was in fact with him when he had the stroke. Now she has joined Aurelius' entourage, where any former Vestal is automatically welcome. I doubt if it means anything, but I thought I better mention her as a person who had access to Verus and now has access to Aurelius. I don't want to leave any stone unturned when the Emperor's life is at stake."

"Good thinking, Brennus. Artemisia, I want you to be with me when I talk to Plautilla."

Artemisia nodded in agreement.

"Brennus, where can I find Plautilla?"

"I think she's at the Imperial villa in Lanuvium at the moment, along with Aurelius himself and others in his entourage. In fact, I think Eclectus is the *cubicularius* at that villa."

"Then we have a plan of action," commented Severus. "I'll talk to the Persian translator here today and then go back to my villa at Lake Nemi. Fortunately, it's only a few miles from the Imperial villa at Lanuvium, so there is easy enough travelling between them.

"Brennus, you can have both Plautilla and Eclectus come to me at my villa. And meanwhile, you will continue to explore the situation. See if you can find others who were with Verus and are now with Aurelius."

Brennus nodded in agreement.

Everyone got up. Flaccus said to Severus "I have to go now to argue my case in front of Judge Memmius. I'll tell you what happened when I next see you." He hurried off.

VII

JANGI, THE PERSIAN TRANSLATOR

At the 9th hour in the early afternoon, the Persian translator appeared at Judge Severus' chambers. The court clerk Proculus ushered him into the room where Severus was seated behind a table, flanked by Alexander and Flaccus, who had returned after his court appearance. The translator was dressed in a formal toga, announcing that he was a Roman citizen. He stood in the room, looking uncertain whether he should remain standing or sit down.

"This is the Persian translator Diogenes," said Proculus.

"Come in, Diogenes. Please be seated. This is my assessor Gaius Flaccus and my secretary Alexander." All three men wore white tunics, Severus' and Flaccus' bearing the narrow reddish-purple stripes of the Equestrian Order. Alexander's had a Greek geometric design in blue on the hems.

"Thank you, *eminentissime*," Diogenes said politely using the Equestrian honorific. "But may I speak Greek? My Latin is not very good."

"Of course," Severus replied in Greek.

"Actually, my full name is Lucius Verianus Diogenes Jangi. Please call me Jangi. Everyone does."

"Lucius Verianus," repeated Severus. "Then you were granted Roman citizenship by Lucius Verus. Is that right, Jangi?"

"Indeed. He was my patron. A great Emperor. A great man. May the gods protect his soul."

"So you have a Roman name now, and a Greek name, Diogenes. But Jangi? Is that a Persian name?"

"Yes, a Persian name. I have the honor of being conversant with three cultures. I was born a free person in the city of Antioch in the province of Syria and I am therefore a citizen of the Empire's 3rd largest city. The name Jangi is a nickname I acquired when I lived in Ctesiphon, the capital of the Parthian Empire. The Persians had trouble pronouncing Diogenes and somehow it came out Jangi, which I like."

"When was that, Jangi?"

"As a child. My father was a merchant, a representative of a Persian carpet firm in Antioch. He toured the country of Iran, as the Persians and Parthians call their country, buying carpets. Our family lived in Ctesiphon for 10 years. I grew up there and I speak fluent Pahlavi, both in the Persian dialect and the Parthian dialect. Pars, the original home of the Persians, as you may know, is in southwest of Iran, while Parthia is in the northeast. When I was 15, we moved back to Antioch."

"How did you become Lucius Verus' translator?"

"By accident, I suppose. When he was in Antioch during the recent war with Parthia, Verus' translator died and he needed a new one. I was recommended and he hired me. I then became not just his client, but his friend and part of his entourage. He brought me back to Rome to continue to advise him on Persian affairs."

"Were you with him when he died?"

"Indeed I was. I was in the coach behind his when he had his attack of *apoplexia*. Terrible. Terrible. He became paralyzed. He couldn't move his limbs. He couldn't talk. The doctor bled him. I thought too much, but I'm no expert. After three days he died. A great person, a great Emperor, a great patron."

"And now, I hear you are part of Marcus Aurelius' entourage. Is that so?"

"Yes, I suppose you could say that. I advise the Emperor on Persian affairs, interpret news from Persia, and help him develop policy toward Persia."

"What I am going to tell you now Jangi is confidential and you are not to tell anyone. Is that clear?"

"Yes, *eminentissime*."

"We have information that Lucius Verus might have been murdered. That his *apoplexia* was not natural but brought on by poison, perhaps. How does that strike you?"

Jangi didn't bat an eye. "I always thought so."

"You did? How come?"

"As far as I could see he was in good health. True, he drank too much, he ate too much, he slept too little and he had a history of illness, I am told. But he was only 39 years old. I know many people die young, that is our fate sometimes, but he was full of life. I don't believe it was natural. I always believed he was poisoned."

"When could that have happened?"

"Possibly at the banquet the night before. I was there, along with others in his entourage. Some musicians, some jugglers, some hangers-on. Which one poisoned him, I don't know."

"I want a list of everyone you remember who was there. Go into the front room and write it out for me."

"I will. But there were maybe 50 people there."

"Just list those you remember. And I want to know what they are doing now. Are any of them part of Marcus Aurelius' entourage today, as you are?"

"I will write it all down for you. I will do anything I can to help out."

"Also, I may call upon you to help in our investigation in the near future. Will you be willing to do so?"

"Oh yes. Of course. I would be happy to. Just tell me what to do, and I will do it."

"Good. Now go into the next room and make a list for me of everyone at the banquet the night before and what happened to them after Verus' death."

"I will do it, *eminentissime*."

Jangi got up and left

Then Flaccus spoke. "How do you know he didn't do it? He may be playing with us."

"Could be. In fact, I have to wonder about his story. He says he is a Greek from Antioch who learned Persian because he lived in Ctesiphon as a boy. But how do we know he isn't really a Persian from Ctesiphon who lived in Antioch as a boy?"

"If he was born in Antioch," suggested Alexander, "his birth may have been registered by his family with the city record office, as is usually done nowadays."

"That's an idea we could check up on," said Flaccus, "although even in the best sailing weather it will take almost 3 weeks to go from Rome to Antioch. With another 3 weeks to return, and time needed to investigate, it may be 2 months before we get an answer that way."

"Then we better start now," concluded Severus. "I'll tell Brennus to give the task to the *cursus publicus*. The Imperial post is fast, or at least as fast as we can expect. But first I want to put the question to Jangi and see what he has to say about it. So bring him back in."

Alexander went out and brought Jangi back in.

Severus gave Jangi a hard stare directly into his eyes. "Sit down, Jangi. I have one question to ask you."

Jangi looked at him inquiringly, then averted the stare.

"It's been suggested that you are not a Greek from Antioch who lived in Ctesiphon as a child, but are a Persian from Ctesiphon who lived in Antioch as a child. How am I to tell which is true?

Jangi made a show of astonishment. "Who could say such a thing? It's absurd. What I told you is true. I am Greek, I am from Antioch and I lived in Ctesiphon as a child."

"How can I confirm that?"

"I suppose you would have to go to Antioch and talk to people there, to members of my family or my friends or acquaintances. You could also check the official records of Antioch. My birth was registered there by my father."

"I will do just that, even though a message to the Prefect of Syria and a reply will take at least 2 months. But thank you, Jangi. That's all."

When he left, Severus, Flaccus and Alexander looked at each other in turn. No one said what was on his mind. So Severus said it. "Let's get that inquiry out as fast as possible? We have to know the truth because if Jangi is from Antioch, as he says, he will likely be loyal to the Greeks of our Imperium. But if is actually a Persian, then he is not only lying to us about his background, but his loyalty will probably be to Persia. It makes a big difference in our investigation. Is he a Greek? Or is he a Persian?"

VIII

AN ASSASSINATION ATTEMPT

Two days later Severus was back in his retirement villa by Lake Nemi. It was a clear, sunny morning and even though it was summer there was a touch of chill in the air. Birds were happily singing and chirping in the garden and beyond, while the family cat Phaon was stalking them. But since he was basically an old house cat who lived in a city, his bird catching skills were minimal.

Severus and Artemisia were lounging on couches together in the garden reading and chatting. Vulso and Straton, Flavia and Alexander were out walking the dog Argos at the lake, punctuating the stroll by throwing sticks into the lake that Argos happily dove in and fetched.

But if it seemed that full retirement was relaxingly back, the idea was broken by the sudden arrival of a chariot of the Imperial Post at the front entrance to the villa. As the charioteer darted out, he was met by the head slave Scorpus who had noticed his arrival. Scorpus escorted the driver through the villa and into the garden. The driver was both tense and sweaty, as if from a hurried and frantic ride.

Scorpus brought him a refreshing cup of *posca*, water mixed with vinegar, which the messenger downed in two quick swallows.

He saluted Severus. "*Eminentissime*, there has been an attempt to assassinate the Emperor. It failed, fortunately, because the Emperor wasn't there. He had been luckily called back to Rome an hour earlier."

"How could there be an attempted assassination if the intended victim wasn't there?"

"I don't know. That's what Brennus told me to tell you. And he asks you come to the villa immediately. I have a chariot outside to take you there."

"Just let me get my toga and I'll be right with you."

Severus went inside, had Scorpus help him wind his purple-red bordered judicial toga around and over his tunic, and joined the charioteer for a ride to the Imperial villa nearby at Lanuvium. First, however, he kissed Artemisia and asked her to follow him to Aurelius' villa in their *carpentum* and bring Alexander, Vulso and Straton with her.

Severus' ride in the chariot was not only too fast for comfort, it was downright harrowing. Every deviation of the road was translated into a bump or shake or jolt or other departure from a smooth ride, while dust flew into the air behind, to the sides, and, as the wind shifted, onto them. Severus hated it, but could do nothing about it. He was happy to arrive at the Imperial villa in well under an hour.

Calling the Imperial villa a villa was an understatement. The place was rather a complex of buildings.

Besides a traditional villa with living quarters for the Emperor and his family, there were other buildings on the grounds as well. There were baths, guest houses, libraries, gymnasia, theaters, a small amphitheater, barracks for the guards and numerous fountains, gardens, courtyards and walkways. Though smaller than Hadrian's huge villa complex at Tibur to the north of the City, the Imperial villa at Lanuvium was more like the six other Imperial villas located throughout Italy. All of them, including the villa at Lanuvium were magnificent, with mosaics, sculptures, paintings and numerous works of art spread inside and outside the complex.

Severus' arrival was greeted by slaves of the villa and he was quickly escorted inside the main building to see Brennus, who was waiting for him. Brennus introduced the *vilicus* Epaphroditus, the person in charge of the whole villa complex. The *vilicus* was an elderly man with a deeply lined face. But the lines and furrows were now amplified by extreme distress and worry. He looked just mortified by what had happened.

"What happened?" asked Severus. "The messenger says there was an assassination attempt on the Emperor even though he wasn't here at the time. How could that be?"

"Come to the Emperor's *cubiculum*, I'll show you."

Severus followed Brennus and Epaphroditus to the door of a large well-appointed bedroom, elegantly decorated, with a comfortable looking bed as the central feature and wall frescoes of plants and birds painted in muted tones of green, blue and yellow. An elegant black and white geometric mosaic decorated the floor.

Brennus halted them at the threshold. "Look."

Severus looked about the room and then something lying at the foot of the bed caught his eye. He reacted. "By Hercules! What is it?"

As he looked more closely, he answered his own question. And tried to hide his sense of horror. There was the body of large snake lying at the foot of the bed. Its head was cut off and lying nearby. The snake was about six feet long, gray, with black rings circling its body.

"It's an asp," answered Brennus. "An Egyptian cobra, a very poisonous snake. It was found in the Emperor's bed, under the covers, evidently waiting for him to take his afternoon nap, which he usually took at the 11th hour. The Fates, the gods, whoever, intervened in the form of a messenger from Rome requiring the Emperor to go there immediately to take care of an important matter. So Aurelius left instead of taking his usual nap, and survived."

"I see. Then the snake must have been put in the bed shortly before the 11th hour. Who could have done it? Who is here?"

"Some members of Aurelius' family, some aides of his entourage. Attendants, functionaries, slaves. Also, some of the people we talked about the other day are here at the villa. The doctor Posidippus is here attending to the Emperor's health, which Aurelius has been complaining about in recent days.

"The Persian translator, Jangi, arrived here a few days ago to consult on current developments with Parthia.

"The former Vestal Plautilla is here as part of the Emperor's entourage.

"Verus' former freedman Eclectus is a *cubicularius* at this villa. In fact, he takes care of this *cubiculum*, this bedroom."

"Interesting," remarked Severus. "By the way, would you happen to know where someone could get an Egyptian cobra, a poisonous snake like that?"

"I have no idea. But I can ask my colleagues in the *curiosi*."

"And I can ask my aides, as well. They'll be here shortly. So let's do that. I want to know where someone could get a snake like that. Possibly we can find the seller, and then, through him, the buyer.

"But for now, tell me who found the snake, when and how it was found, and who killed it."

"I'll bring you Eclectus. He can answer those questions, I believe."

Brennus went to get Eclectus, while the *vilicus* escorted Severus to the Latin library in the villa and into its spacious reading room with scrolls in cubbyhole shelves and excellent bronze statuary on stands and tables, along with a desk and chairs. Wine and fruit were brought in for the judge to refresh himself before beginning his interviews. At the same time his own *carpentum* drew up with Artemisia, Alexander, Vulso and Straton. They joined the judge, who first suggested they be taken to see the snake on the floor of the *cubiculum*. After viewing the crime scene, they took seats in the Latin library for fruit, wine and to participate in the questioning to follow.

IX

THE *CUBICULARIUS* ECLECTUS, A CLEANING SLAVE AND THE PRAETORIAN LOTHAR ARE QUESTIONED

Brennus led in a thin, clever-looking man, with suspicious eyes, a sharp pointed nose and tight lips. "This is Eclectus, the *cubicularius.*"

"Sit down, Eclectus," began Severus, "and tell me what happened. Did you find the snake?"

Eclectus sat down, looking tense and more than a little wary, as he took in the presence of a judge in his magistrate's toga along with four others, all obviously sizing him up.

"I didn't find the snake myself. It was found by one of the female slaves who was tidying up the bedroom for the emperor's nap."

"Her name?"

"Cynthia."

"Go on."

"She screamed and everyone in the area came running, including me. She had drawn the covers back and exposed the snake. One of the Emperor's body-guards who was here, came in, unsheathed his sword and beheaded the creature."

"His name?"

"I don't know his Roman name. But his German name is Lothar. He's here at the villa."

"Before I talk to them, Eclectus, tell me when you were last in that bedroom before the snake was found?

"I was there in the morning to get the Emperor out of bed, as he's asked me to do. He likes to stay under the covers as long as possible and says he would stay there all day if he could. Anyway, I'm to wake him at the 1st hour of the morning, and that's what I did. I also put out his clothes for the morning and help him with his toga on days he is wearing it."

"When did you find out that the Emperor had left for Rome?"

"I didn't know that he had left or when he left until after the snake was found and someone said he had left about an hour before."

"Eclectus, how long have you been one of the Emperor's *cubicularii*?"

"Only for a few months. Before that I was with Lucius Verus as one of his *cubicularii*. I was a member of his *familia*. I previously was a slave and then a freedman of Verus' father."

"How did you happen to become part of Aurelius' entourage. I know he let most of Verus' freedmen go. Why did he take you on?"

"I don't know. Perhaps Verus had some good words to say about me when he was alive. I am reputed to be especially efficient and capable and smart. So that may be why."

"Were you with Lucius Verus when he died?"

"I was, yes. I was in one of the coaches in his entourage when he was stricken."

"What happened to him, in your opinion?"

"I don't know. They say he had apoplexy. People get it all the time, even people as young as Lucius Verus. But I'm not a doctor. I don't know. Not that that doctor Posidippus, the one who bled him, knows either."

"Are you saying that the doctor made a mistake in bleeding him?"

"I don't know. But that's what some people say. Maybe it's just gossip. But maybe not."

"Why would the doctor do that?"

"Because of Antonia, his wife. Because she threw herself at Lucius Verus and the Emperor wasn't averse."

"How do you know this?"

"I was one of his *cubicularii*. I know who went into his bedroom. And Antonia made more than one appearance there when her husband wasn't around and the Emperor summoned her."

"Thank you Eclectus. You may go."

Severus turned to Brennus. "Bring in Cynthia. And then Lothar."

"What do you think?" the judge asked generally of the aides who were with him.

Alexander spoke up first. "The doctor told us it wasn't true that Lucius Verus and his wife had been together. Now Eclectus is telling us that it was true. If so, then the doctor has a motive."

"Agreed," replied Severus, "unless Eclectus is lying in order to provide the doctor with a motive."

Then Brennus came back in leading a frightened looking young girl. She was wearing the standard gray tunic and head kerchief of the numerous cleaning slaves always going up and down the corridors. She was hunched over and wary.

"Don't be frightened Cynthia," began the judge, who understood her body language. "Nothing bad is going to happen to you. Just tell us what happened with the snake."

"*Eminentissime*, I went in to straighten up the *cubiculum* for the Emperor's nap. I didn't know he had left the villa. I thought he would be taking his afternoon siesta, as usual. I saw some sort of movement under the blankets on the bed. I thought I was seeing things, but I drew back the covers anyway and I saw that thing in the bed. That horrible snake. I screamed and called for help. Then other people came into the room and I left. That's all."

"Thank you, Cynthia."

She left and Brennus brought in the bodyguard Lothar. He was tall, well-built, strong and had blue eyes and blonde hair. A German, without doubt. He also had large ears. He saluted the judge.

"Your name?"

"Lothar. It's my German name. My Roman name is Manlius Caespe, but my real name is Lothar. I am a German, a Batavian. I am one of the *equites singulares Augusti*, a Praetorian cavalryman, a bodyguard of the Emperor."

Lothar stared steadily at his questioner. Severus was undecided whether his blank look concealed his thoughts or whether he might not have any thoughts to conceal.

"Tell us what happened this afternoon."

"I heard a scream coming from the direction of the Emperor's bedroom. I rushed in, as did a number of others who heard the scream, and saw Cynthia pointing at the bed. In the bed was a snake, a gray one with black stripes around its body. I knew it was an Egyptian asp. Poisonous. I had seen one once before when I was in the East with Lucius Verus, whose bodyguard I was when he was alive. Anyway, I immediately drew my sword, threw off the covers, and beheaded the thing."

"Did you know that the Emperor had left the villa for Rome sometime before?"

"Certainly. Two other *equites* went with him to Rome as his guards, while I was told to stay here along with one other guard because the Emperor would be returning, although no one knew when. We would take up guarding duties on the shift of bodyguards when he came back."

"You say you were with Lucius Verus in the East. That was during the war with Parthia, was it?"

"Yes, you can say that. Though except for one time when we went to the front for appearance's sake, I was mostly in Antioch, or in Daphne, Antioch's pleasure garden, because that's where the Emperor was, having a good time. I was one of his guards then and I was also one of his guards when he died. I was on a horse riding at the side of his coach when he was stricken."

"What do you think happened to him?"

"He had a stroke, just as the doctor said. It was natural. No one murdered him, as some of the gossip-mongers allege. No one murdered him on my watch. That I can tell you. It was all natural."

"Thank you, Lothar."

Lothar saluted and left.

"So?" asked Severus casting glances at his entourage, one after another.

Brennus spoke up. "Lothar is another one who was with Verus and is now with Aurelius. According to your theory, judge, he should be an automatic suspect."

"Quite true, Brennus. Quite true."

"So now," said Vulso summing things up. "We have the following suspects who were with Lucius Verus and are now with Marcus Aurelius. Posidippus the doctor. Jangi the Persian translator. Eclectus the *cubicularius*. And now Lothar, the bodyguard."

"Don't forget the Vestal Virgin," reminded Artemisia, "or should I say the former Vestal."

"Yes," interjected Brennus. "What about her? She's here at the villa at the moment."

"Then we might as well talk to her now," said Severus. "Bring her in."

Severus turned to Vulso and Straton. "I want you both to head back to Rome immediately and buy an Egyptian cobra."

"What?" exclaimed Vulso. "I have no idea where to buy one."

"Neither do I," agreed Straton.

"I have no idea either," replied Severus. "So I'm giving you the job of finding out. I'm sure you will."

Vulso and Straton shrugged, saluted and left the library.

X

SEVERUS AND ARTEMISIA TALK TO PLAUTILLA, A FORMER VESTAL VIRGIN

"It's a pleasure to meet you, Judge Severus," began Plautilla as she took a seat opposite Severus and Artemisia. "The Emperor has spoken so highly of you. Both Emperors, as a matter of fact."

"Thank you for saying so, Plautilla. It is very gratifying."

A bowl of fruit and cups and beakers of wine were on the table between them.

Plautilla was a tall, handsome looking woman, with shrewd eyes and a smile that was sometimes ingratiating and sometimes sardonic. She looked like there was not much you could put past her. Her hair had been elaborately coiffured by an *ornatrix* and she wore a beige tunic with a green belt and green geometric designs on the hems of the sleeves and skirt. It was an expensive tunic as was obvious because it shimmered as only the best silk from distant Seres could.

She wore a gold snake bracelet coiled around her upper left arm.

"It is also an unexpected pleasure and honor to meet you, Artemisia," continued Plautilla. "I have read your biography of Cleopatra and enjoyed it immensely. I am a great admirer of your work, of your writing style and of your understanding of history and the people involved. A very perspicacious work. I would be honored if I could discuss it with you when we are finished with whatever it is the judge wants to talk to me about."

"Thank you, Plautilla. Not that many people have read it that I know of. It's very gratifying just to come across someone who has."

"Vestal Virgins read a lot. There isn't much else to do," said Plautilla with one of her sardonic smiles. "But not only is your biography historically interesting, evidently it is currently relevant, is it not? After all, Cleopatra committed suicide by letting a poisonous asp bite her and just today, I hear, there was a poisonous asp in the Emperor's bed."

"Is that why you're wearing a snake armlet," asked Severus, looking directly at her jewelry.

She laughed. "I thought it timely to wear it, yes."

Severus gave her a doubtful look. "In any case, Plautilla, I'm told that you were with Lucius Verus when he died. Am I correctly informed?"

"Yes, you are. In fact, I was in the *carpentum* with him when he had the stroke. We were talking and all of a sudden a strange, far-away look came over him, he started to babble, to talk incoherently, and collapsed. I yelled at the coachman to stop and called for a doctor. Posidippus came and examined Verus who was stretched out on the ground and seemed paralyzed, unable to talk at all. It was frightening."

"How was it that you were in the coach with Verus, may I ask? It was coming back to Rome from the war front in the north, wasn't it?"

"Yes. I joined Verus in Alsium by pre-arrangement. You see, we were good friends by that time." She gave both Severus and Artemisia a knowing look. "Yes. Friends is an understatement, you realize."

Both Severus and Artemisia looked at her with inquiring expressions.

"Let me tell you about it. You see, I was 'captured', that's the word the Vestals use when they take new children into their service, I was 'captured' at the age of 7. New recruits are always between the ages of 6 and 10. They have to have noble Roman citizens for fathers, and they have to be unblemished. We have to serve as Vestals for 30 years. The first 10 years are spent in training, the next 10 in duties, the last 10 in teaching new recruits. There are only 18 Vestals at any one time, 6 in their first decade, 6 in the second, and 6 in the third.

"Our basic duties, as everyone knows, are to keep the perpetual flame from going out, and to appear at various ceremonies and at gladiatorial games and chariot races. We get the best front seats.

"After 30 years we are released from service to Vesta and are allowed to lead a normal life, get married, have children. One of the constant discussions among those in their last decade is whether and how to lose our virginity when we leave the cult. Some never do, some are only too anxious to get out and get on with a real life.

"As for me, I decided that I definitely wanted to lose my virginity. The question was 'who with'. Ex Vestal Virgins are much in demand and we can therefore make our own choices. I decided to lose my virginity with an Emperor. I was told that Marcus Aurelius was seriously married, begetting children one after another, and didn't play around. However, Lucius Verus played around all the time. It was notorious that he had a wild affair with the beautiful Panthea when he was in the East. Anyway, I contrived an introduction to him and made obvious my desire. He was most happy to oblige. We were then together, on and off, for the first 6 months after my release.

"At his death, I decided to try my luck with Marcus Aurelius. As a former Vestal and an intimate of Lucius Verus I am totally welcome into the Imperial entourage. But as I said Aurelius is very married and besides, he seems more interested in deciding legal cases than he is in me."

"I'm glad to hear," commented Severus, "that the Emperor gives priority to duty and service to the law, although I have never doubted it."

"In any case," said Plautilla, "the Emperor has mentioned to me that you're trying to find a possible Persian assassin. He thinks the whole idea is just 'smoke', but after yesterday's attempt on his life, I suppose it must be given credence. So I for one, will tell you who that assassin is."

"Who is it?"

"It's that Persian translator, Jangi. I didn't trust him when he was with Lucius Verus and I don't trust him now. He speaks both Greek and Persian fluently. He says he is a Greek from Antioch who learned Persian because he spent a few years as a child with his father's carpet business in Persia, in Ctesiphon. Isn't that what he's told you?"

"Yes."

"But how do you know if it's true? How do you know he isn't really a Persian who spent a few years as a child in Antioch in his father's carpet business there?"

"You have a good point, Plautilla. And we've already thought about it and have started checking up on his story. As for now, you can go and I thank you for your forthrightness."

She rose and beckoned to Artemisia. "Would you come with me, Artemisia, and have something to eat and talk about Cleopatra."

"I would like that," Artemisia replied as she got up to join Plautilla in leaving the room.

Brennus came in when the women left.

"Well. What do you think?" said the *curiosi* agent.

"Brennus, send a message to the Emperor. He is not to return to this villa. It's too dangerous. There's an assassin on the loose here. I will send him a letter to that affect as well.

"And also confine everyone at the villa here until further notice. Attendants, servants, guests, slaves, everyone. No one leaves the villa until I say so."

"But how do I do that? What should I tell them?"

"You can tell them it's by my order. I want everyone to stay here except the Emperor. If anyone objects, send them to me."

"Do you want the suspects incommunicado with the outside? Completely cut off?"

Severus thought a moment. "No. I want them to be able to send and receive messages, letters. And I want to intercept them. Can you station a few *curiosi* agents at the villa with a number of copyists? All messages to and from any of the suspects must be intercepted, read and copied. If the *curiosi* agent in charge decides to let them be delivered they will. But in any case, I'll want a copy of all correspondence whether they seem relevant or not, incriminating or not. Also, I would want the messengers who deliver messages to be questioned by the *curiosi* and I want *curiosi* agents to deliver outgoing messages and learn what happens when they arrive. Can you arrange that?"

"I don't see why not," replied Brennus, who saluted and was about to leave, but stopped to say something to Severus, who was taking a large quaff of wine.

"Judge, there is something I want to say about this assassination attempt." Severus looked at him inquiringly.

"As far as I'm concerned it's definitely the *spasaka* behind it. I say that because of what was accomplished. You might think on the surface that the attempt was a failure. Maybe even a clumsy failure. The snake didn't even get to bite the Emperor. But the Iranians are subtle, as it is often said. They might not have killed the Emperor, but they have reached right into his bedroom. And planted something horrible in his bed. A snake. A creature most people are afraid of, both rationally and irrationally. They have in fact struck fear into all of us. What's next? Maybe poisonous spiders? Maybe poisoned mushrooms? Maybe an arrow launched from a rooftop? Maybe a Persian assassin in the Praetorian Guard? Who knows? And that's just the point. To put fear into the heart of the Emperor. It may even be more important than killing him. For fear of the Persians must now enter the Emperor's mind when he devises policy toward Persia. Fear of the Persians must now enter into his mind when he enters his own bedroom. Maybe not on the surface of the mind of a Stoic like Aurelius, but underneath, where we all have irrational, uncontrollable fears. The *spasaka* knows that. And that, in some basic way, may be the real purpose of this assassination attempt. Maybe even more important that killing the Emperor is making him afraid of you."

Severus understood precisely what Brennus was telling him. A threat is often stronger than its execution. This phenomenon was familiar to Severus as a strong player of the strategy and tactics board game of *latrunculi*, The reason a threat is often stronger than its execution is because of how it may affect the other player, who may see other threats or often overestimate its power. He fears what the move might do rather than what it does objectively. And that fear can lead him astray. His own imagination can undo him.

"I understand exactly. It is a subtle but real effect." Severus paused and asked Brennus another question. "So you see the hand of the *spasaka* in this, do you?"

"I do. I definitely do."

"Does the *curiosi* do the same sort of thing?"

"I won't answer that," replied Brennus with a crooked smile. "But my own preference for assassination is the poisoned needle."

"How does that work?"

"Someone developed the idea during the reign of Domitian about 75 years ago – maybe earlier, I don't know – during his purges. You dip the head of a needle into poison and prick a person with it. In a crowd is best. You can walk by the victim, prick him with the needle in passing and leave, unnoticed. The victim hardly feels anything and doesn't even know what he's died of. Of course, you have to get close to the victim and that's not so easy to do with an Emperor."

Brennus saluted again and left.

Later that day, Severus asked his wife how her lunch and discussion with Plautilla went.

"Did she seem knowledgeable? What kind of person was she?"

"She was knowledgeable all right. She read my book and we had an interesting discussion about Cleopatra. I told her that I had started a new book, a biography of Aspasia. And she was knowledgeable about her too, knowing she was the lover and consort of Pericles, that they had a child together, that she ran an intellectual salon and that Socrates had said she was the only person in Athens who could best him in dialogue and wit."

"That's interesting."

"Not as interesting as what then happened."

"Oh?"

"After lunch we went to her room and she tried to seduce me."

"Oh?"

"Yes. A little clumsily, I have to say, but when I didn't respond, she openly propositioned me.

"I told her that I have a pact with my husband. We don't engage in extramarital sex. We are persuaded by philosophers such as Musonius Rufus that extramarital sex weakens marriage, causes conflict and interferes with relationships. Faithfulness, on the other hand, strengthens a marriage, strengthens companionship, strengthens love. Avoiding outside temptations also conforms to one of the main precepts of Stoicism, *temperantia*, self-control."

"What did she say to that?"

"She said that as far as she was concerned, she had enough of self-control as a Vestal Virgin. Now she favored the pursuit of pleasure with no restraints. In fact, she said she had no restrictions about anything. She did whatever she wanted. And that was that."

"That snake armlet she was wearing. What did you think of that? Did she wear it as a challenge to me, as if to say she had something to do with the assassination attempt, but there's nothing I can do about it? Or was it something else?"

"Snake bracelets are very common, of course. I have one, as you know. But as to why she wore it? I just don't know. It may have been a challenge or just a joke on her part. She seems to be doing whatever she wants, unconcerned by what others think.

"But there's something more I want to report. After I left her room, I realized I had left behind a scroll I had been carrying and so went back to retrieve it. But as I turned a corner into her corridor, I saw that big Batavian cavalryman entering her room."

"Lothar?"

"Yes. Him. I waited more than a few moments to see if he was coming out, but he didn't. I even snuck up to her door and heard loud sounds of laughter and then soft sounds of intimacy. So I suspect he was going to spend some time with her in the pursuit of pleasure, as she called it."

"So those two are together in some way. Maybe just as lovers, but it creates a suspicion that they may be conspirators."

"Conspiring to assassinate?"

"Maybe."

"Why?"

"Persian gold, perhaps?"

"Persian gold? But she's a Vestal. He's a Praetorian. Both should be loyal to the State, to the Emperor. Or do I misread the loyalties of you Romans?"

"Loyalty to the State may be a fortification against betrayal, it's true, but isn't it sometimes said that 'there is no fortification that cannot be captured by money'?"

"I've heard that before."

"Well, we must keep it in mind now."

XI

A LETTER TO THE EMPEROR

Marcus Flavius Severus to Marcus Aurelius
Antoninus Augustus. Greetings:

Domine, I am writing to inform you about the
progress of the investigation into whether a Persian
assassin in on the loose, intending to kill you. While
we always thought there was some possibility that the
report from the *curiosi* agent inside Persia was inaccu-
rate or just misinformation or disinformation, we can
no longer entertain those ideas.

Someone attempted to assassinate you yesterday
by placing a poisonous snake, an Egyptian cobra,
in your bed in anticipation of your afternoon siesta.
Fortunately, you were called away just in time. This
means, for one thing, that you must stay away from
the villa in Lanuvium. It is too dangerous.

Since the person who placed the snake in your bed
must be someone at the Lanuvium villa, I have ordered everyone there to be confined to the villa. No
one leaves without my permission.

I have been working under the assumption that the Persian assassin murdered Lucius Verus. That may or may not be true. But if it is, I have further assumed that the assassin is someone who was with Verus' entourage at the time of his death, and who is now part of your entourage. These people are automatic suspects to be investigated.

So far, I have found 5 people who meet that criterion. There is the doctor Posidippus, the Persian translator Jangi, the *cubicularius* Eclectus, the Batavian bodyguard of the *equites singulares Augusti* Lothar, and the former Vestal virgin Plautilla. There may be others yet to be discovered who also meet the criterion. If you know of any besides the ones I've mentioned, let me know immediately.

The assassin may be one of these or none of them, but these top the list because of opportunity. As to motive, there may be personal reasons involved or it may be Persian gold at work. Or both.

While it may be difficult to believe any one of these suspects is a Persian assassin, that they may appear to be entirely innocent, bear in mind that skilled assassins may be trained and clever in concealing their true colors.

Vale.

/seal/ Marcus Flavius Severus

SCROLL III

XII

HUNTING FOR AN
EGYPTIAN COBRA

Where do you find a poisonous Egyptian cobra? That was the question Vulso and Straton asked themselves as they sat in a room in the Castra Praetoria, the headquarters of both the Praetorian Guard and their own Urban Cohort.

"This is Rome," said Vulso out loud. "You can find anything here." He took a sip of wine from a cup on the table in front of him.

"Maybe so. But where do we start?"

"Maybe the expert from the Imperial zoological collection can tell us. Where is he anyway? He was supposed to be here by now."

Just then a slim man in a copious toga too big for him came into the room and greeted Vulso and Straton. "My name is Lucius Claudius Anxius. I'm an assistant curator of the Imperial zoological collection. I'm sorry to be late, but there was an awful traffic jam this morning on the Vicus Patricius. Seems like a litter overturned and then there was an altercation. Traffic was snarled. People pushing and shoving and yelling and cursing. The usual morning traffic nightmare. But I'm here and I'm told you can use my help."

"We hope so", replied Vulso, motioning Anxius to a chair at the table and gesturing that he should have some wine that was in front of him. "We hope you can tell us where we can find a poisonous Egyptian cobra."

"Poisonous, you say? That's a challenge." Anxius had some wine but hardly skipped a beat before he went into a lecture about snakes. "Snakes are not that uncommon in Rome. Many people even keep them as pets. The Emperor Tiberius had one he fed with his own hand."

"You sure he wasn't feeding himself," interjected Straton.

Anxius made a little smile and continued. "Seneca once wrote about a tame snake slithering along the table at a dinner party. But those snakes were not poisonous, of course. So where would I find a poisonous snake? Well, there are a number of zoological collections in the City. Besides the Imperial collection, some wealthy animal enthusiasts have them. But I don't know whether they include poisonous snakes. I suspect they don't. But who knows? We could visit one of these collectors and ask him. Maybe he knows what other collectors have. Maybe one of them will know. And I know one not far away, a short walk from here.

"His name is Decimus Dentatus. An Equestrian. And very, very rich. He lives nearby on the Viminal Hill, where he has a large *domus* and a zoological park on the premises. Let's send him a message that the

Urban Cohort wants to speak with him this morning about a matter of some urgency and importance."

Anxius took out a wax tablet and a stylus from a fold in his toga and wrote a message on it, while Vulso called for a slave messenger to take the tablet as fast as he could to Dentatus' Viminal Hill *domus*.

About an hour later, the messenger returned with the second leaf of the wax tablet inscribed with a reply from Dentatus and handed it to Vulso.

"He says we can come any time," read Vulso. "So let's go now." He turned back to the messenger. "Run ahead and tell Dentatus we're on on our way now."

The slave left and Vulso, Anxius and Straton headed out of the Castra and walked toward the Viminal Hill. Fortunately, it was not far away because this was the second day of a heat wave and Rome's temperature, air pollution and disagreeable smells were all rising, along with the irritability of the population. Outside of buildings the air was oppressive; inside stifling.

They were met at the *domus* of Dentatus by a number of obsequious slaves who escorted them into the *tablinum* of the *domus* where Denatatus was seated at a table. He rose, pointed them to seats on the other side of the table.

Dentatus was short and fat, scruffy and unsavory looking. His hair was long and unkempt. His beard and eyebrows were bushy. His tunic was of the finest linen, but it had visible food stains all over it. He looked sort of creepy.

On the table was a large turtle, some cut up carrots and a bowl of water. A large black ferocious looking

Molossian hound sat next to Dentatus' chair, eyeing
the visitors suspiciously. An orange cat was curled up
in one corner of the room, watching. A colorful red
and yellow parrot was on a perch in a cage in another
corner, also watching.

"I love animals" were Dentatus' first words. "It's
people I can't stand."

"Why is that?" asked Vulso, amused by Dentatus'
unusual description of himself.

"Why? You ask why? Look at this turtle on
the table. He is satisfied with a few vegetables and
fruits and water. He doesn't kill anyone. All right,
maybe an insect or two. But he's gentle. Even wild
animals are gentle compared to people. Can you
imagine the Flavian amphitheater full of 50,000
turtles watching other turtles kill each other? Can
you imagine thousands of turtles lined up in battle
formation ready to kill each other? No. Not turtles,
not even lions. Lions may take down other animals
for food, but lions don't wage war, they don't enjoy
watching other lions killed. Birds don't commit ex-
tortion, bribery, or arson. Rabbits don't lie, cheat
or steal. So that's why I can't stand people. People
are horrible murderers and criminals. But animals?
Never."

"You make a good point," said Vulso, "though I
should point out that turtles are not capable of building the Flavian amphitheater."

"That's just my point," shot back Dentatus, whose
voice was becoming harsher and face getting redder
by the moment. "Even if turtles could build an amphitheater, they wouldn't want to. Only people can

build it and then use it to kill themselves and animals as well. That's why I love animals and detest people."

"I have to agree with you," commented Anxius solemnly.

"So you're in luck," put in Vulso, "because just now we're here to talk about animals. Snakes in particular."

"Snakes?" Dentatus' face lit up. "I have snakes. Monkeys, too. And dogs and cats and birds. And toads and turtles and rabbits. Come, I'll show you."

He half rose from his seat but saw that Vulso held up his hand as if to restrain him and sat back down.

"We would love to see all your animals, but first I need to call on your expertise."

Dentatus looked expectantly at him.

"Do you have or have you ever had any poisonous Egyptian cobras?"

"Me? Poisonous cobras? What for? I have non-poisonous snakes. And if I ever had a poisonous snake it would have to be tamed not to bite anyone. Snakes are a symbol of health. That's why a snake is coiled around the rod of Asklepios, the symbol of doctors. But why would I have any poisonous ones?"

"Do you know anyone who has some? Do you know where I can find a poisonous Egyptian cobra, for instance?"

"Off hand, I don't know anyone in Rome. But I do know one place that is sure to have poisonous snakes."

"Where is that?" asked Vulso.

"The Marsic priests."

"Who are they?" asked Straton.

"Snake charmers. They serve the goddess Angitia, a goddess of healing. The Marsic priests turn poisonous snakes into harmless snakes that won't bite anyone. I don't know how exactly. They have their secret methods, though I've heard they use massages and incantations, maybe even music. But that's what that cult does. I'm thinking they probably have Egyptian cobras and they probably import them from Egypt. Whether they sell or give them away or what they do with them, I don't know.

"Of course, maybe you can find such snakes in Rome. Probably you can because you can find almost anything here. Sometimes you see snake charmers in gathering places around the City playing flute music to entice snakes out of a basket, but I don't believe those snakes are poisonous. I don't really know, though, and I don't know anyone who has untamed poisonous snakes. So the Marsic priests are your best bet."

"Where are they located?"

"In central Italia. In the Apennine mountains. At the town of Marruvium. By Lake Fucinus."

"That's quite a trip," commented Vulso.

Denatus just shrugged his shoulders.

The visitors got up with Anxius saying, "now we would love to see your menagerie. Your snakes in particular."

Dentatus and his dog escorted his visitors outside to his animal garden and they spent a while looking at the collection. Anxius was particularly interested in the animals, asked a lot of questions and exchanged zoological information with Dentatus, who enjoyed every minute of the tour he was giving. He described and petted every animal in his collection. He picked up each snake gently and identified it for his guests. His whole manner exuded a love for his animals and all his animals seemed to love him in return. He concluded his tour with a comment.

"You can't even imagine 50,000 snakes seated in an amphitheater watching other snakes kill each other, can you?"

"No," replied Vulso. "I can't imagine it."

When they left, walking back to the Castra Praetoria, Straton turned to Vulso. "I'll go to the Marsic priests."

Vulso, who wasn't at all interested in making an arduous trip to the mountains, smiled and replied, "good plan, Straton, good plan."

XIII

STRATON TRAVELS TO
THE MARSIC CULT AND
MAKES A DISCOVERY

At the 1ˢᵗ hour of morning the next day, Straton boarded a four horse *carpentum* coach belonging to the Urban Cohort and headed east out of Rome toward the Apennine mountains. He carried an official letter from Judge Severus as *iudex select*us of the Emperor to the head priest of the Marsic cult, introducing Straton as his representative and asking for cooperation. It was a matter of urgency and importance to the Emperor personally, the note said.

It took Straton more than a day and a half to reach the temple of the Marsic priests by Lake Fucinus. The ride itself was bumpy because there was no major road leading there. But the scenery was beautiful, even inspiring, as the coach went up into the mountains which offered a panoramic view of the landscape from the heights. Farmland, vineyards, and the lush summer greenery of the rolling hills of Italy were as bracing as the wonderful mountain air.

As an emissary on a mission of importance to the Emperor himself, Straton was dressed in civilian clothes, with his citizen's toga over a tunic. While he often acted a part in an undercover capacity, his guises were mostly of ordinary people. His sad brown eyes fostered deception, blending him into a crowd and making him virtually invisible. In the past, Straton had taken the part of a poor philosopher wandering the City, a coach driver on the roads outside Rome, a devotee of Isis, a mourner at a funeral, among other disguises. Now he was not just a soldier of in the Urban Cohort, not just a staff member of a judge of the Urban Prefect, but a special representative of the Emperor's special judge. A man of importance and influence. He could be somewhat haughty, although not arrogant. His wishes had to be accommodated without question. The sad eyes would have to change their aspect. But Straton was a good actor.

On this mission, Straton was accompanied by a slave of the Urban Cohort named Pectillus. He also had a role to play. He was tall and strong and looked authoritative, even intimidating. His tunic was expensive, made of the finest linen, displaying wealth and taste. His presence and demeanor were to make Straton look very important.

But while they radiated the look of elite Romans, their talk was mostly about slavery. Straton had been a slave of the Emperor Hadrian as a young child and was freed upon the Emperor's death. Though young, he had never forgotten the indignities of slavery.

"I know you were once a slave," said Pectillus. "I know you hate slavery. Your story is told among the slaves of the Urban Cohort. So I know you have taken the initiative, when possible, in freeing slaves of the Urban Cohort."

"That's true. But I've only been able to free one slave. His name is Pinna, and I obtained freedom for him by choosing him to become a spy in our investigation in the case of the Return of Spartacus. It was a dangerous assignment and freedom was his payment for volunteering to risk his life."

"Is it possible that this role I am playing now can lead to my freedom?"

"I really don't think so. There is no risk involved. If it were my choice, of course, I would free all the slaves. But it's not up to me. As you know, in our society many freedmen who were once slaves own slaves. There are even slaves who themselves own slaves. However, I will keep you in mind, if you want, for any dangerous roles that may arise. Will that do?"

"It will have to do, I suppose. I hate being a slave. I just hate it."

"I know. I know."

It was around midday that they arrived at the Temple of the Marsic priests. It was an old and rustic temple, plain without much embellishment. When the coach drew up, Pectillus got out and went into the temple to announce the arrival of an emissary of the Emperor's special judge. Straton remained in the *carpentum* while Pectillus presented the letter from Judge Severus to a greeter inside the temple. He, in turn, immediately went somewhere out of sight while Pectillus waited. Soon a priest with a number of slaves came into the temple, greeted Pectillus, and headed outside to offer a formal welcome to the emissary. Upon their appearance, the coach driver rushed to open the door of the coach for Straton. He emerged, looked around in a slightly superior manner, sniffed the air, and then returned greetings to the priest.

"Welcome, welcome," said the priest. He wore a complicated robe, with an ample portion covering his head in the manner of religious devotion. He had a long white beard. "My name is Teucer. I am the chief assistant to the high priest of the Marsic cult. Please come inside and enjoy refreshments after your long, arduous trip. The high priest himself will join you."

Straton thanked Teucer and followed him into the temple, into a side room where slaves were laying out fruit and wine on a table. Immediately, another priest entered the room, dressed in the same way as Teucer, even to having a similar long white beard. He introduced himself as Paternus. "Welcome. I am the high priest of the Marsic cult and anything I can do to aid the special judge help the Emperor, I will certainly do. Just ask."

"I was sent," began Straton who drank a draught of wine, "to make inquiries about your snakes."

Paternus looked at him inquiringly.

"First we wish to know whether you have here any poisonous Egyptian cobras?"

"Yes. Of course. We import them from Egypt and tame them through our special snake charming methods. That is what our cult does. These snakes, when tamed, bring health, make people whole by their presence, and carry forth the message of the goddess Angitia, the goddess of healing."

"Do you ever sell them before they are tamed? While they are still dangerous?"

"Never, willingly. Our snakes are tamed and employed in healing. For instance, some Aesculapian health centers have our snakes slithering around the floors of their hospitals. Some private citizens who believe in the healing properties of our tamed snakes have them at home. But it does occur, though rarely, that we are required to sell poisonous, untamed snakes."

"What do you mean by that? Who requires you to sell these poisonous snakes while untamed?"

"Well, only recently we received a visit from a *munerarius*, a producer of arena shows, at the Flavian amphitheater. He wanted two poisonous Egyptian cobras for the noon executions of criminals at the next games at the amphitheater."

"What was the name of the *munerarius*?"

"Gaius Obesus was his name."

"Obesus?" exclaimed Straton. "Was he very fat or was that a family name or what?"

"He was obese. The name suited him. Anyway, he explained that people were becoming jaded with the usual executions by lions or bears or panthers. He wanted something new. He said his idea was to put a criminal in a sack with a biting, poisonous snake, seal them up together, and put the sack in the center of the arena. He was sure, he said, that the crowd would love watching the sack move every which way, as the criminal tried unsuccessfully to avoid the attack of the snake. The crowd would find it very humorous, he thought. Obesus himself laughed at the idea of it. It would be a grand show, he said.

"We gave him what he wanted. And he paid us very well for the two snakes."

"Two?"

"Yes, two. Both very healthy snakes, untamed and very poisonous. He had a slave with him who seemed to know about cobras and who made the choice."

"Did he make a good choice?"

"Indeed, he did. He seemed to have some expertise about snakes. In fact, I think from their talk that it was the slave's idea to use the snakes, not the *munerarius*."

"What makes you say that?"

The two priests looked at each other and smiled. Paternus replied. "The slave was a very beautiful young man, with olive skin, dark, almost black eyes, and lithe body movements, almost like a woman. He seemed able to twist the *munerarius* around his finger. Obesus agreed with everything he said. And then they spent the night here and slept together. The sounds were unmistakable."

"What was the name of that young slave?"

"I've forgotten," replied Paternus. He looked at Teucer. "Do you remember?"

"Yes. I do. It was a Persian name, wasn't it? Nush, I believe. They mentioned something about him being captured in the recent war, enslaved, and bought by Obesus. Nush is Obesus' slave and also his lover."

"A Persian," exclaimed Straton. "What do you know about that? A Persian."

It went without saying that Judge Severus would be very interested in that. So after a good dinner, a good night's sleep, at dawn the next morning Straton and Pectillus boarded their coach and headed back to Rome as quickly as possible.

XIV

SEVERUS QUESTIONS THE
MUNERARIUS AND HIS SLAVE

Straton arrived at the Forum of Augusts around noon on the day after he left Lake Fucinus. He found Judge Severus in his chambers playing a game of Latrunculi with Alexander. The heat wave was still ongoing in the City and both players were sweating and mopping their brows with handkerchiefs as the game progressed. A court slave had been sent in with a large peacock-feather fan. Desultorily, he fanned the players for some time, but had to leave, himself almost dropping from the heat.

As for the game, no matter how much Alexander had studied and practiced, he was still unable to beat Severus, though he had managed to draw a few times. It was in the end, perhaps, a matter of aptitude and talent, imagination and calculation. The game in progress was as usual clearly going the judge's way and Alexander was close to resigning. He was saved for the moment by Straton's arrival.

"I have something very interesting to report," began Straton.

Vulso was in the anteroom with court clerk Quintus Proculus and they both came in to hear the report. Everyone listened attentively and without questions to Straton's concise recounting of what he had learned at the Marsic cult. Hardly had Straton concluded than the judge issued orders.

"Vulso, immediately gather a *contubernium* of the Urban Cohort, go to the Flavian amphitheater and arrest the *munerarius* Gaius Obesus and his Persian slave Nush. If they're not there, find out where they live and go there. But find them and bring them here under guard. The charge is attempted murder of the Emperor. They brought back two Egyptian cobras from the Marsic cult. I'm theorizing, though of course I don't know for sure, that one of those snakes was the one in the Emperor's bed in Lanuvium. As for the other cobra, find it and impound it. Go."

Vulso bolted out of the room without comment.

"Straton, you looked tired. Take a nap on the couch outside so you can be here when Obesus and Nush are brought in."

Straton went to the couch in the anteroom and crashed.

Then Severus turned to Alexander. "You're not going to get out of our game so fast," he said. "It's your move, isn't it?"

"Yes. But I resign."

"The proper response," replied the judge. "You are improving, I have to say. Our games are becoming more interesting all the time. So keep at it."

"I'm not sure I'll ever beat you, judge."

"Not many people have. I'm not sure why. It's not a matter of intelligence. Many intelligent people are just not very good at games. But for some unknown reason, I have an aptitude for games. I must have been born with it. Games come naturally to me. Not just Latrunculi. I'm good even at dice games, at Tabula, at the Sacred Way, at almost any game. But I'm best at Latrunculi.

"Anyway, right now, I want to wait for Vulso to bring in the *munerarius* and his slave-lover. I have a few hundred questions for them."

Two hours later Vulso returned to Severus' chambers. "I've brought back two snakes, one an Egyptian cobra, the other a person."

"Which one, the *munerarius* Obesus or his Persian slave Nush?

"Obesus. Only he's not really the *munerarius* responsible for producing the Games. He's an assistant to the *munerarius*, an aide for the production of the midday executions. We found him in his *insula* apartment on the Aventine Hill."

"What about Nush?"

"We know where he is and will pick him up later today. He's at a dinner in a *Mitharaeum*, one of those centers for the worship of the Persian god Mithra. It's in a private home of a Mithra follower a few streets from where Obesus lives. We have the *Mithraeum* staked out and we have someone who can identify Nush. As soon as he comes out, we'll arrest him and he'll be brought here."

"Good work, Vulso. Now wake Straton and bring him in. I want both of you here for the interrogation. Then bring in Obesus."

"I should mention that Obesus, besides being very fat, is totally distraught, almost on the verge of tears. And frightened. I told him he's charged with attempting to kill the Emperor. He blubbers that he doesn't know what this is all about or what's happening to him. He denies everything."

"Bring him in."

Vulso went out. Straton and Proculus then came in and took seats around the table in Severus' chambers. Then Vulso dragged Obesus into the room by the scruff of his neck and pushed him down in a chair across from Severus. He was a very fat man with a weak chin, weak eyes and a weak voice. He was also sweating profusely.

"What did I do? I didn't do anything," Obesus wailed. "Why am I arrested? I didn't do anything."

Severus looked him over. "Obesus. Is that your nickname or a family name?"

"A family name. My father was obese, my grandfather was obese. I'm obese. But I don't know why. I don't eat very much." He grabbed a bunch of grapes from the fruit bowl on the table in front of him and gobbled them down.

Severus then glared at him hostilely and spoke to him in a forceful voice. "I am Marcus Flavius Severus, *iudex selectus* investigating an attempt to assassinate the Emperor. You bought two poisonous Egyptian cobras from the Marsic cult, didn't you?" accused Severus. Obesus shook. "Didn't you?"

Obesus drew a handkerchief from a fold in his toga and wiped his sweating brow. "Yes, *eminentissime*. I did. I bought the snakes for the Games. For the midday executions. That's all I did. What's wrong with that? That's my job. What is this all about? I didn't do anything wrong. There must be some mistake."

Severus proceeded to interrogate Obesus following his theory that the cobra in the Emperor's bed was one of the snakes Obesus bought from the Marsic cult. For effect, the judge stated it as a fact.

"Obesus, one of those cobras was used in an attempt to assassinate the Emperor. The attempt failed, fortunately. But that cobra was yours. You bought it, so you are a perpetrator of the assassination attempt. Under the *lex maiestatis*, you are guilty of treason and face the death penalty and forfeiture of all your property. In addition, even though a citizen, you can be tortured for evidence, your slaves can be tortured and they can give evidence against you. Also your name is subject to *damnatio* forever."

"But I didn't do anything," he sniveled. "*Eminentissime*, please help me. I am innocent of everything."

"I just told you what you did. Now you tell me why you purchased those snakes. But I want you to tell me how come one of them was used to try to kill the Emperor?"

"But I don't know anything. All I know is that I got the two snakes to use at the noon executions during the next Games." His manner became imploring. "They were for the purposes of executing criminals, not assassinating the Emperor. Please. I didn't do anything wrong."

"Start from the beginning. Whose idea was it to use snakes in the noon executions?"

"It was my idea. I remembered the old horrible punishment for parricide, of putting the murderer in a sack with a dog, a rooster, a snake and a monkey and throwing the sack into water. I thought I might leave out the dog, the monkey and the rooster and exhibit the sack in the arena with the condemned criminal and a poisonous snake. The crowd would laugh themselves silly when they saw the sack moving this way and that with the criminal trying to avoid the snake. I bought the snakes for that purpose and even told the Marsic priests that it was my idea to put a criminal in a sack with a poisonous, biting snake." Now his manner was ingratiating, though what he was saying repulsive.

Straton interrupted. "The Marsic high priest told me that he thought it might have been your slave Nush who thought up the idea. He thought Nush had some experience in handling and choosing the snakes. So was it his idea or yours?"

Tears came into Obesus' eyes. He wiped them with his handkerchief. "No. It was my idea. Not his. He has nothing to do with this, except I got the idea because he once told me he had some experience in handling snakes in Persia."

"What happened to the snakes? Only one was found today. How did the other get out of your care to be used in an assassination?"

"I don't know." He hesitated. "Maybe it escaped on its own."

"And crawled all the way to Lanuvium? Get serious, Obesus. I want my question answered. How did that snake get to be used the way it was? Did you give it to someone? Or did Nush?"

"I don't know, *eminentissime*. Nush took charge of both snakes. I never saw them after we brought them into the basement of the amphitheater to store until the next Games. I didn't know one was missing at all. I don't know anything. I didn't do anything. Please, *eminentissime*. Please let me go. I'm innocent. I'm sure Nush is innocent too. Let me go, I beg you."

"Tell me about Nush? When did you buy him? Where?"

"I bought him from a friend who lives nearby. Actually, it's the person who has the *Mithraeum* in his house, where Nush is having dinner tonight. He saw I was taken with Nush and sold him to me at a reasonable price. This was six months ago."

"What is your friend's name?"

"Publius Plautius Pudens. He and his family are members of the Senatorial Order."

"That will be all for now, Obesus." Severus looked at Vulso. "Put him in a room with a guard at the door." Turning back to Obesus. "You'll stay under arrest at least until I talk to Nush."

Vulso dragged Obesus out of the chair and out of the room and deposited him in a room with a member of the Urban Cohort guarding the door.

About an hour later, four soldiers of the Urban Cohort came to the judge's chambers with Nush. The slave looked terrified, glancing this way and that, as if seeking help. They brought him into the judge's chambers and threw him into the same chair that Obesus had occupied an hour before.

Severus looked him over. There was no doubt about his physical beauty. Deep, melting black eyes. Olive skin. Perfect teeth. Lithe, perfectly proportioned body. Exceptionally handsome features. Almost feminine grace.

"You are the slave Nush, a Persian, the property of Gaius Obesus?"

Nush nodded affirmatively.

"Speak up."

"I am Nush, a Persian," he replied in heavily accented Latin.

"Do you speak Greek?"

"Better than Latin, *kyrie*" he said in Greek.

Severus switched to Greek. "You are charged with attempting to assassinate the Emperor. The attempt failed, but it was attempted with an Egyptian cobra, one of the ones your master and you obtained from the Marsic cult. It was one of the cobras put in your care. How did that cobra end up in an assassination attempt? What do you have to say about this?"

Nush seemed to collect himself. He tried to turn on the charm he knew he possessed. "I know nothing about it, *kyrie*. I put the snakes in the storeroom in the amphitheater and never saw them again. That's the truth." He smiled beautifully, but unconvincingly.

"I don't believe you. You were in charge of those snakes. If you never saw them again, what happened? Did you tell anyone about the snakes?"

"Yes. Yes. I told everyone. I must have told at least 10 people. One of them must have stolen the snake you're talking about. I had nothing to do with the snake being missing. As far as I know, the snakes are still in the storeroom. I was going to attend to them when the next Games neared. But that's not for a few weeks yet. After I put the snakes into the storeroom, I never saw them again. Someone else gave them their food and water. Not me. I swear it, *kyrie*. I swear it by all the gods, the Persian gods, the Greek gods and the Roman gods."

He relaxed back into his chair with a self-satisfied smile.

He didn't stay that way for long. "Unfortunately, Nush," shot back Severus. "I have no reason to believe you. Maybe you're telling the truth, or maybe not. So I suppose I will have to order you to be interrogated under torture. Then we will find out what really happened."

His whole demeanor changed. "Torture? No. No. I'm telling the truth. There's no need for torture, *kyrie*." He literally squirmed in his seat.

"Who are the 10 people you told about the snakes?"

"Well, I don't know exactly. They were people working at the amphitheater. Workers, slaves. I don't know their names. I never knew them. But I told them. I swear, *kyrie*. I swear."

"I can't accept your explanation. It's too vague. Let's see what your story is under torture.

"Vulso, put him in a room with a guard.

"Nush, you can think about things overnight. If I don't get a better explanation of how the snake got from the amphitheater in Rome to be used in an assassination attempt in Lanuvium, I will order you tortured for evidence.

"Vulso, take him out."

Fear was visible on Nush' face when Vulso lifted him up roughly by his hair and dragged him out of the room.

"Are you really going to order him tortured?" asked court clerk Proculus. "You usually set little store by torture. Too much lying to stop the pain."

"I know. But let Nush stew overnight at the prospect of undergoing torture. I'll have to stew overnight with the prospect of ordering it."

XV

SEVERUS VISITS A *MITHRAEUM*

The next morning Severus was at his chambers in the Forum of Augustus by the 2nd hour. He had decided to postpone for another day the decision of whether to order the torture of Nush. However, he would have Nush brought into the room with all the instruments of torture displayed to intimidate him to see if he would talk without actual torture. If he did, well and good. If not, he could stew for another day under threat.

In any case, Severus wanted to visit the home of Publius Pudens, the member of the Senatorial Class who had sold Nush to Obesus and who had a *Mithraeum* in his home on the Aventine Hill. Maybe he could find out more about both Nush and Obesus, while exploring just what a Roman aristocrat was doing as a devoted follower of the Persian god Mithra. Where did Pudens stand with regard to the recent war between Rome and Parthia? How much a captive was he of the Persian god? Did he know about the

Egyptian cobras in the care of Nush and Obesus? So Severus instructed his court clerk Proculus, who always was at his post by the 1st hour, to send a message to Pudens announcing that the judge would visit him today at the 5th hour, if it would not be inconvenient for him. If not, he could suggest a time, but it would have to be today. Matters were urgent and Severus was a *iudex selectus* appointed by the Emperor himself. My investigation takes priority over all other business.

Within the hour, a return message was received from Pudens, inviting the judge to come at the 5th hour, as he had proposed.

Since it had rained the night before, the heat wave had broken and it was a nice, warm summer morning, prompting Severus to walk to the Aventine Hill residence of Pudens. The *domus* was close to the Circus Maximus and Severus, along with Vulso, Straton and Alexander, took one of his favorite routes out of the Forum of Augustus, through the Forum of Julius Caesar, through the Old Forum Romanum, along the Sacred Way to exit that Forum and then circle beneath the Palatine to the Circus Maximus. There were no chariot races scheduled at the Circus that day, so it was open as a thriving market and already very busy as Severus passed through. Besides food stalls selling meats, vegetables, fish, grains and spices, there were numerous shops of various kinds, copper ware, pottery, statuary, antiques and sundries. There were musicians playing lyres or flutes, some accompanied by singers, and there were barbers and doctors, jugglers and acrobats. There were storytellers gathering listeners with their traditional call, "give me a bronze coin and I will tell you a golden story."

The whole scene not only appealed to Severus for displaying the vibrant life of the great City, which he liked to feel himself a part of, but it took his mind off the case, even for a little while. That was relaxing.

Eventually, Severus and his aides traversed the 2/5 of a mile length of the race track, exited and walked to a street near the house of Pudens on the Aventine. There, by prearrangement, they were met by an 8-bearer litter of the Court of the Urban Prefect. Severus climbed aboard and was carried in state for an impressive arrival at Pudens' house, a Roman magistrate decked out in his judicial red-purple bordered toga. Vulso, Straton and Alexander accompanied the litter on foot, the members of the Urban Cohort themselves decked out in their impressive military uniforms. Vulso's centurion's helmet, with the transverse side to side crest, displayed his impressive rank.

The litter was met by slaves in front of Pudens' domus, who were prepared for the visit. They helped Severus exit the litter, making sure that his judicial toga was not sullied by touching the ground. As Severus descended, Pudens himself appeared. He was of medium height, but thin, almost emaciated looking, with sunken cheeks and boney fingers. He also had a rather unhealthy grayish pallor about him, with a rigid face, a sourpuss, unsmiling, with cold eyes. Severus didn't like him at first sight, but the two politely exchanged greeting kisses in the Roman style.

"Welcome to my home, Judge Severus. It is an honor to receive such a distinguished emissary of the Emperor." There was sarcasm in his voice.

"And I am also honored to greet a member of the Senatorial Order who I hope and expect will help me in this investigation which is of so much concern to the Emperor personally."

Severus was escorted into the house and brought into the *tablinum* office of Pudens, where a table was already set up with bowls of fruit and pitchers of wine and water. Slaves poured the liquid mixture into beautiful transparent glassware, which showed off the full-bodied color of the red wine being served.

"A Massic," said Pudens.

"One of my favorites," replied Severus politely, and truthfully.

Pudens was also dressed in a formal toga, with the broad red-purple stripe of the Senatorial Class on his tunic showing through, a contrast to Severus' narrow stripe of the Equestrian Class. However much the Senatorial Order outranked the Equestrian Order, in this case the judge's magistrate's status took precedence over anyone else except another magistrate.

"I am here," began Severus, looking Pudens straight in the eye, "to investigate an attempt to assassinate the Emperor."

He paused but Pudens made no comment, so the judge continued.

"A friend of yours, Gaius Obesus, an aide to the *munerarius,* and his slave Nush, who was once your slave, are, I regret to say, deeply involved. They are at risk of being executed under the *Lex Maiestatis*."

"I can't believe they're guilty of anything. What did they do?" His tone of voice expressed doubt and challenge.

"They bought two Egyptian cobras from the Marsic cult, ostensibly to use in the midday executions at the next Games. However, I believe one of these cobras was actually used in an attempt to assassinate the Emperor. Someone placed that cobra in the Emperor's bed in his villa at Lanuvium. Fortunately, the Emperor had been called away earlier that afternoon and never encountered the poisonous snake. The cobra was discovered and killed. Since Obesus and Nush were in charge of that snake in Rome, they are on the hook, so to speak, because there is no explanation of how the snake ended up in the Emperor's bed in Lanuvium except by an act of Obesus or Nush, or both. They may have delivered the snake there themselves, or given it to someone else, who brought it to Lanuvium and put it in the Emperor's bed. Whatever the case, they are implicated in the plot and will be duly executed unless I can discover some other explanation showing their innocence."

Severus took a sip of wine and waited for Pudens to reply.

"As I say, I can't believe it. Someone must have stolen the snake. What do they say?"

"Obesus says he doesn't know anything about it. He says he didn't see the snakes after they were placed in the storeroom of the amphitheater. Nush says the same thing, He also says he told a number people about the snakes, but he can't or won't say who."

"Well?"

"Well, I have no reason to believe them. Nush in particular is vague and unconvincing. I will likely order him, and maybe Obesus as well, to be tortured for evidence."

"But Obesus is a citizen. He can't be tortured, isn't that so, judge?"

"This is not the Republic. Under the *Lex Maiestatis*, anyone, citizen or not, can be tortured when treason is the crime, let alone assassinating the Emperor. "

"I see."

"By the way, I understand you once owned Nush and that he is a follower of Mithra, as you are. Even yesterday, I understand, he was here for dinner at a gathering of Mithra followers. Is that so?"

"Yes, it is. I have a grotto excavated in one of the rooms of this *domus*. Grottos are the place for Mithra rites, dinners, and other ceremonies. I would show you, judge, but the grotto is open only to devotees and members of the Mithra cult. Are you perhaps a member?"

"No."

"Then I hope you will be satisfied with my talking about the grotto, rather than seeing it."

"For the time being, at least. As a magistrate, a *iudex selectus*, I can order your grotto to be opened to myself and my aides. You understand?"

"So you say." His tone became hostile. "But I must tell you, judge, that I also have access to the Emperor and perhaps he will countermand any such violation of my religious sanctuary."

"Is that so?"

"Yes."

"We will return to that issue shortly. First, I want to know a few things about the Mithra cult and then about the slave Nush."

Pudens looked at him expectantly.

"What was the position of the cult of Mithra during our recent war with Parthia? Mithra is a Persian god, isn't he?"

"Yes, he is a Persian god originally. But the worship of Mithra is very popular, particularly among members of the Roman military, who call the god Mithras. But I prefer the original Persian name, Mithra. The Mithra cult doesn't admit women, for one thing, and there are blood sacrifices, for another. Bull's blood, especially. Roman soldiers like blood. But the Roman followers of Mithra support Rome, not Parthia, and we pray for the health of the Emperor and make sacrifices of incense in his honor. We are not like those Christian atheists who don't believe in the gods and refuse to make patriotic sacrifices of incense in honor of the Emperor and the Empire. Roman followers of Mithra are loyal to Rome."

"That is your official position, I know. But aren't there some Mithra followers who are not quite so sure of their loyalties?"

"None I know of."

Severus was skeptical, but continued his inquiry. "Now tell me about Nush? How and where did you buy him? Why did you sell him to Obesus? And since he is a Persian, I want to know what his loyalties are."

"Nush is but a mere boy. Very beautiful, as you must have noticed. I bought him at the slave market in the Saepta Julia in the City about a year ago. He was taken captive during the recent war. His beauty was his main attraction, if you know what I mean. I had to outbid a number of other people. I sold him to Obesus about six months ago because I was tired of him and Obesus was smitten. That's all."

"He seems to have known some things about snakes because he chose the snakes Obesus bought and was put in charge of them. Do you know about that?"

"No. He never mentioned snakes when he was my slave and I know nothing much about his background. It wasn't of interest to me. He was just a slave, after all. Not a person."

"Is that the way you feel about all your slaves?"

"More or less. Although various girls and boys may become of some interest for a short time. But that's all."

"So, Pudens, now tell me about your influence with the Emperor? I wish no clashes to occur between us over things like precedence, authority, *et cetera*." Severus' manner was deferential, although he was being disingenuous. Severus was confident in his own authority not only as a special judge, but even more so in his personal friendship with the Emperor.

"For one thing," replied Pudens with a certain haughtiness, "my sister is a member of his entourage and close to the Emperor. She is a Vestal Virgin, though one whose 30-year term has expired, but she is of the highest, noblest character, chaste and of religious eminence. The Emperor hangs on her very word."

Severus thought a moment. "If I am correctly informed, your *gens* is Plautius, isn't that right? You are Publius Plautius Pudens. So your sister must be called after your father's and your *gens* name. Just like my daughter is Flavia, after my *gens* name Flavius, your sister must be Plautia, yes?"

"Plautilla, in her case."

"Oh, Plautilla? I think I have met her."

"Then you must know of her exemplary, chaste and religious character. One especially commending itself to our philosophic, Stoic Emperor."

Her chastity, thought Severus to himself, trying to keep himself from laughing. Yes I know about that. Mistress to Lucius Verus, attempted seducer of his own wife, lover of the member of the *Singulares*, Lothar, and who knew who else.

"Thank you for your cooperation, Pudens. I will take what you say into consideration. But I am still of a mind to order judicial torture because frankly I don't believe Nush or Obesus. If you want to visit them and maybe help in getting them to tell the truth without torture, I invite you to come to the Forum of Augustus and see them. But it must be today. Because tomorrow I will set up my Tribunal and carry out judicial torture if they are not more forthcoming."

With that Severus had a last sip of wine, stood up, and left the *tablinum*, heading back to his litter. He boarded it, was carried one street away, then got out, dismissed the litter bearers and the litter and walked with Vulso, Straton and Alexander, recounting his interview with Pudens.

"His sister is Plautilla?" laughed Vulso. "The vestal nymph, as she's now being called."

"More importantly, is the connection. It's possible, isn't it, that the snake was delivered to Plautilla by Obesus or Nush or even Pudens. This whole connection is highly suspicious. One of our main suspects, Plautilla, is now directly linked to the people who bought the snake used in the assassination attempt."

"If Pudens is himself involved," commented Alexander, "maybe he will visit Obesus or Nush and try to fabricate a story for all of them to tell."

"I'm hoping he will," replied Severus. "That's why I invited him to come to our courthouse and talk to them. Pressure on all of them will perhaps lead to them making mistakes, stumbling in their attempt to deceive us. So let's see if he shows up today. And then I must talk to Plautilla again. She is more of a suspect now than before."

By late afternoon, Pudens showed up in the Forum of Augustus, asking to see first Obesus and then Nush, both imprisoned in guarded rooms.

When Severus was informed by his court clerk, he smiled broadly. "Escort him to the prisoners in the order he wants to see them. Then he will probably want to see me. When he does, show him right in. I'll be very interested to hear what he has to say, to hear what they have concocted."

XVI

WHAT PUBLIUS PUDENS SAID

Judge Severus waited in his chambers for Pudens to visit the prisoners Obesus and Nush and then come back to him with a story. It was already the 1st night hour when Pudens began, so Severus had dinner ordered into his chambers from the restaurant Subura, located just behind the Forum of Augustus at the entrance to the Subura section of the City. It was a favorite lunch spot for court personnel and still open for dinner.

Severus invited Vulso, Straton, Alexander and Proculus to dine with him, while court slaves fetched their food. A patina of red mullets cooked in wine with pepper for the judge; anchovies with eggs for Straton; asparagus in wine, pepper, coriander and salty *liquamen* dressing for Alexander; Lucanian sausages with pepper, cumin and *liquamen* for Vulso; green beans in a sweet and sour sauce of mustard, honey, cumin and vinegar for Proculus. Both red and white wines were served with the food

Lively conversation accompanied the meal, with talk turning from chariot racing to Greek literature to the latest theater productions in the City. Talk of the case, of crime, of the law was somehow avoided, a silent conspiracy among the diners.

As they were finishing with a dessert of figs, dates and apples, Pudens returned and asked to see the judge. He was invited in join everyone for dessert and wine and asked then and there to say what he wanted to say. Pudens looked at everyone having a good time and in a jolly mood, saw that no one was going to leave, had a sip of wine and began.

"Judge, I've talked with both Obesus and Nush. After much convincing on my part, the slave finally confided in me. He told me the whole story, the truthful story. And I can say without reservation that you will not have to torture him. He is relieved to tell the truth."

"I'm happy to hear that," said Severus. "What did he have to say?"

"He admitted that he was the person who stole the missing Egyptian cobra. He said he sold it to a worker at the amphitheater for 5 gold aurei."

"Is that so? What was the name of the person he sold the snake to?"

"He doesn't know the man's name, but he can identify him by sight if he sees him."

"What did he do with the money?"

"He spent it all on food, on wine, on brothels."

"And what about Obesus? What added light did he have to shine on this story?"

"Nothing. He never saw the snakes after they were put in storage. I, it goes without saying, knew nothing about any of this. It is all the fault of the slave, Nush, as he will now freely admit to you. You will get the same confession with torture or without it. So in the name of humanity and mercy, I ask you not to torture him. He's admits his crime."

Severus looked at his aides. "Did you ever hear such drivel?" He turned to Pudens. "You expect me to believe this? It's pure *nugax*, nonsense."

"But judge, I...."

"Shut up, Pudens, and now listen to me. You are not sufficiently aware of your position personally. First, the *Lex Maiestatis*. Do you want me to read the law to you? Or do you know that the attempt to assassinate an Emperor is covered by it. And do you know that anyone, of any class, Senatorial, Equestrian, any citizen can be tortured for information? Do you know that anyone implicated can have his property forfeited, his name condemned to *damnatio*, and be executed?"

"I know that."

"Then appreciate the following. That Egyptian cobra you're talking about was found in the Emperor's bed in his villa in Lanuvium, a good 20 miles from Rome. There are only a few people who had access to the Emperor's *cubiculum*, one of whom was your sister Plautilla. So the snake was in Rome in the care of your former slave and fellow Mithra cult member Nush and your close friend Gaius Obesus. The obvious inference is that *you* had the snake delivered to your sister, either personally or by an agent, and conspired with her to kill the Emperor."

"But, but....."

Severus cut off his coming protest. "Get out of here. And come back only if you can address those issues with a story that makes sense. A vague, concocted story putting all the blame on some unfortunate slave will not do. Now get out."

Pudens stood up. He pointed a boney finger at the judge. "I'm a member of the Senatorial Order. My father was an actual member of the Senate. I am entitled to more respect from you, a mere Equestrian. I will personally write to the Emperor, telling him of this outrage. You will hear from him."

"Is that so? Sit down then." Severus wanted to snap off the finger Pudens was pointing at him, but remembered the Stoic principle of *temperantia*, self-control, and instead addressed his court clerk. "Quintus, bring writing material and take a letter in shorthand." Pudens sat down, a suspicious, even worried, look coming to his thin face. Proculus returned with a wax tablet and stylus and nodded to the judge to begin.

"Marcus Flavius Severus to Marcus Aurelius Antoninus Augustus. Greetings:

Domine. I have before me as I write this letter a member of the Senatorial Order named Publius Plautius Pudens. He is deeply implicated in the attempt to assassinate you. In the matter of the snake found in your bed, he is connected to the two people, let me call them his underlings, who purchased the snake from the Marsic cult. He has also proffered an absurd story to explain away his involvement. In addition, his sister is Plautilla, a former Vestal, who is in your entourage and also was a member of your brother Lucius' entourage when he died. Therefore, she must now become a prime suspect.

When Pudens is confronted with suspicions against him flowing naturally from the facts, he refuses to tell a coherent, convincing story. Instead he has tried to put all the blame on a poor slave.

Now he says he will write to you, calling conclusions backed up by facts an 'outrage.'

I trust you will answer his letter by letting him know the realities of his situation.

Your life-long friend, devoted citizen and personally selected special judge, Marcus.

Vale."

Severus turned to Pudens, whose face was visibly pale. "Now get out."

Without a further word, Pudens left.

"Do you really want me to send this letter to the Emperor?"

"Of course not." Severus smiled. "It was only for effect."

Everyone began to laugh. "What will happen now?" asked Vulso. "Are you still going to torture the slave tomorrow?"

"No. I've decided to change tactics. I will see if I can get the truth from Nush by kindness, not cruelty."

XVII

WHAT NUSH SAID

At the 3rd hour the next morning, Vulso escorted Nush into Severus' chambers. He sat down across the table from the judge. He was shaking with fear, expecting to be tortured. But the table had a bowl filled with fruit, figs, dates and grapes, and carafes of wine and water. Severus indicated to Nush to help himself. Without hesitation, the slave gathered as many fruits as he could in his hands and virtually wolfed them down. He then gulped down wine, and then helped himself to more fruit.

When his hunger and thirst were slaked, fear returned to his face. Severus put on a soft, gentle manner and talked to him sympathetically.

"Nush, I am not going to have you tortured. Instead I'm going to free you from the control of Obesus and Pudens. From now on, you will be a slave of the Court of the Urban Prefect. While you will still be a slave, you will not be the powerless plaything of unscrupulous and lustful owners. You will…"

Severus hesitated.   Nush was weeping, at first barely, but then profusely, tears flowing down his face. Severus passed a handkerchief across the table to him. Nush used it to wipe his face, but the tears continued unabated. Finally he got control of himself.

"Thank you. Oh, thank you. Thank you." He began to cry again. There were tears of relief and tears of joy. When he dried his eyes once more, he said. "I am so grateful to you. You can't even know how much. You are my savior. My Mithra. Anything you want to know, just ask. I want to tell you everything."

"Tell me what happened with the missing Egyptian cobra?"

"I don't know exactly, *kyrie*. The day after the snakes were put in the storeroom of the amphitheater, I went down to look after them." He dabbed his wet eyes and face with the handkerchief. "I brought their food with me. My master Obesus and my previous master Pudens were both down there discussing the snakes. They saw me and told me to choose one of the snakes and put it back into the wicker basket they had there. I needed help to handle the snake and Obesus called over another slave, Hercules. His name is a joke on him because he is very small. So I held the snake from behind its neck, as I was taught to do, while Hercules held its back and tail and we put him in the wicker basket. You can ask Hercules."

"I will, Nush. Tell me what happened next."

"Then Pudens told me to bring the basket with the snake and come with him. Obesus told me that I was now on loan to Pudens for a few days and I must do anything he wanted. So I went with Pudens along with the snake back to his house on the Aventine Hill, where I had been a slave before Pudens sold me to Obesus. Pudens told me that we were going on a trip in the *carpentum* the next day with his secretary and a six of his slaves. That night he raped me."

Nush started to cry again. "It's not that it never happened before. It happened all the time when I was his slave. But while Obesus also had his way with me, he was gentler about it. Pudens is brutal and I was back in his clutches. I was in despair."

"What happened the next day?"

"The next day we boarded two *carpenta*, one for Pudens and his secretary Dendron and…"

"Dendron? Greek for 'tree'. Is that his real name?"

"No. It is a nickname because Pudens thinks he looks like a tree. His arms and legs and fingers are like sticks. Pudens gives everyone nicknames, mostly demeaning, humiliating ones."

"But you're still called by your real name, Nush, aren't you?"

"Now. Yes. My master Obesus allows me to use my real name. But when I was the slave of Pudens he called me by an obscene name." Nush hesitated, then spoke. "He called me 'Posterior'. I hated it. But that's why he used it."

"I'm sorry. But please continue your account of the trip to Lanuvium."

"As I was saying, there were two *carpenta*. One for the master and his secretary Dendron. The other was for the slaves, including me and the snake basket, which was tied on top of the coach. I knew all the slaves from when I was a slave in the same household.

Pudens told me not to mention what was in the basket to anyone. So I didn't."

"What were the names of the other slaves on the trip?"

"There were Delta, Epsilon, Mu, Rho, Iota and kappa. Iota and Kappa were the drivers, the others were litter bearers and also did odd jobs like cleaning, whatever Pudens wanted. The litter was carried on top of our coach."

"Did you know where you were going?"

"I didn't. But Epsilon said we were going to Lanuvium to visit Pudens' sister. That's the talk he had overheard. We were all there – the litter, the litter bearers – to make an impressive appearance."

"What happened when you arrived at Lanuvium?"

"I don't really know. I was kept in the slave quarters of a guest house and wasn't allowed out anywhere. I was responsible for taking care of the snake, feeding it, *et cetera*, and that's what I did. I don't know what Pudens did or who he met. The litter bearers took him places, but they didn't really know either. They said he went off with other people and they were just hanging about waiting for him to return."

"What happened to the snake?"

"Two days after we arrived, someone took the basket away. I never saw or was told who it was. The next day we returned to Rome. That night he raped me again and the next day he returned me to Obesus. Judge, my savior, I want to help you any way I can. Just ask. I…" His eyes once more welled up with tears.

Severus raised his hand to slow him down. But Nush couldn't stop talking. He was grateful to the judge as his savior and poured out his grief at what had happened to him as a slave. "At one moment I was a free boy in Persia living with my family – my mother, my father, my sisters and brothers – the next I was a slave of the Romans subjected to rape, to indiscriminate lusts, to beatings, to horrors I can barely describe. But now, you have come to my rescue. My prayers to Mithra have been answered."

"I'm not sure that Mithra had anything to do with it, Nush. But I am happy to help you. My aide Straton, who was himself once a slave, will escort you to the Castra Praetoria, where the Urban Cohort is based. You will be put into the slave pool there. You will still be a slave, but you will be well treated.

"But before you go, I would like to know what Pudens said to you yesterday when he visited you in the prison room?"

"He told me to say nothing about the trip to Lanuvium. He threatened to torture and kill me if I did. He said he would get me back from Obesus and torture me worse than anything you would do to me. But now I don't care. You are not going torture me and you will free me from the control of those horrible masters. I don't fear him now. I revere you."

"Thank you, Nush. One final question, though. How did you learn about snakes, about handling them?"

"From my father, in Persia. His job was to capture snakes and give them to those who used them for health reasons. Just like in Greece, Persians believe snakes are symbols of health. So I learned as a child how to handle snakes."

Severus then rose, went to the door of his chambers and called Straton in, asking him to take Nush to the Castra Praetoria.

"Did your new tactic work?" asked Straton.

"It worked beautifully."

Then Severus called Vulso over and asked him to go to the Flavian amphitheater and find a slave named Hercules. "He is very small. I want him brought to me immediately"

Within two hours, Vulso returned with Hercules. He was questioned by the judge about what happened to the missing Egyptian cobra and confirmed what Nush had said. He himself had been told by Obesus to help Nush put the snake in a wicker basket, close the top, and give the basket to Pudens, which he had done. He added, "another slave named Demetrios was also there and saw the whole thing, that is, me and Nush putting the snake into the basket and Nush going off with Pudens and the snake basket."

Severus directed Vulso to find the slave Demetrios. Within the hour he was in front of the judge and confirmed what Hercules had said.

That was enough. Severus then instructed his court clerk to send a messenger to Pudens at his *domus* on the Aventine Hill. "The message is to say that Pudens is ordered to appear five days from today at the 3rd morning hour at my Tribunal in the Forum of Augustus. This is to be considered a 5-day notice of trial. The charge is violation of the *Lex Maiestatis.*"

"What about Obesus? Is he going to be a defendant too?" asked Proculus.

"Maybe. But first I will try to make him one of my witnesses against Pudens. According to Nush, Hercules and Demetrios, Obesus was there when the snake was handed over to Pudens. He can testify to that. If he refuses, if he lies, then he will become a defendant."

Severus started to pace the floor of his chambers, his hands clasped behind his back. "We now know how the cobra got from Rome to Lanuvium. Pudens took it. But we don't know who Pudens gave it to. Presumably it was that person who put the snake in the Emperor's bed."

"Didn't he give the snake to his sister?" said Vulso. "It must have been her. She is the Persian assassin."

"She is a likely suspect, of course. But we have no evidence against her that we can use at a trial. Perhaps Pudens used his connection with his sister to visit the Imperial villa, while his true purpose was to give the snake to someone else. We don't really know."

"So how do we proceed?" asked Proculus.

"First of all, I'll keep the pressure on Pudens. Maybe he'll talk, though I doubt it."

"It's a treason case," said Proculus. "You could use torture on him."

"Legally I can. But I'm always suspicious of the truth of what anyone says under torture. Besides, Pudens is a member of the Senatorial Class and there will be many people who object to the use of torture on the upper classes, legal or not.

"No. What I want to do is prepare for the trial in the next 5 days. Eventually I'll have to return to Lanuvium and question Plautilla and the other suspects again. But first the trial. Vulso, tomorrow I want you to bring Pudens secretary Dendron here along with the six slaves Nush mentioned. The ones whose names are letters of the Greek alphabet. Maybe I can get more information from them. They were all at Lanuvium and maybe they saw or overheard something useful."

"Who will be the prosecutor?" asked Proculus.

"I'm thinking of Flaccus."

"But he's usually your assessor."

"Yes. But he's been practicing law on his own since my so-called retirement started. Send him a message to come here tomorrow morning. I'll see if he's available and wants to come in as the prosecutor. Maybe he'd rather be my assessor on the Tribunal instead."

"One other question before I leave," said Vulso. "What do we do with the other cobra, the one we've impounded?"

"I don't know," replied Severus. "Any suggestions?"

"I have one," answered Vulso. "I'd like to give it to Dentatus, that animal lover who has his own zoological collection at his villa on the Viminal Hill."

"Do you think he'll love this poisonous cobra?"

"He probably will."

"All right. Arrange it. Anything else?"

Everyone shook their head, no.

"Then it's on to the trial of Pudens for treason."

SCROLL IV

XVIII

PRE-TRIAL PREPERATIONS

The next day a lawyer representing Publius Pudens appeared at Severus' chambers asking to speak to the *iudex selectus*. Upon coming into Severus' chambers and seeing the judge, both Severus and the lawyer exclaimed almost in unison, "Not you again?" They smiled at each other and exchanged greeting kisses in the Roman style.

The lawyer was Claudius Cassius Casca, who had appeared before Judge Severus a few months ago as the defense lawyer for the arch criminal Gnaeus Bulla. Casca was a large, impressive looking man, with a belligerent lower lip, two chins, a potbelly and a deep, impressive voice. He was known in the courts as a skilled advocate and a persuasive orator who deservedly obtained important clients and commanded high fees. He was also a member of the Senatorial Order and the gap in his toga prominently displayed the broad purple-red stripe on his tunic.

"I heard you retired, *eminentissime*," began Casca. "But apparently you haven't."

"Actually, I have, *clarissime*. I'm no longer on the panel of judges for the Court of the Urban Prefect. I even retired to a villa in the countryside. But as luck would have it, I've been called out of retirement by the Emperor, appointed *iudex selectus* and asked to investigate an attempt to assassinate him."

"Has there been an attempt? I haven't heard of any."

"Yes, there has been one. And there is evidence that your client Pudens is implicated in it. That's why I've scheduled him for trial under the *Lex Maiestatis*."

"I find this all hard to believe. My client is a member of the Senatorial Order and not a traitor. So would you mind telling me what the facts are? What was the attempt and what evidence there is that my client is involved?"

"Not at all. I'd be glad to."

Severus then launched in some detail into the assassination attempt. "I will leave out for the moment the role of the *curiosi* in coming up with information about an assassination, and focus on your client's role in having an Egyptian cobra put in the Emperor's bed in Lanuvium. It seems he procured that cobra from his friend Gaius Obesus, who is an aide to the *munerarius* for Games at the Flavian amphitheater. Obesus had purchased the snake ostensibly to use in the midday executions, but actually gave it to Pudens.

"Pudens then personally transported the snake from Rome to Lanuvium and gave it to someone there, who put it into the Emperor's bed. Possibly that person was his sister Plautilla, who is part of the Emperor's entourage and whom he was visiting. You can see, Casca, how deeply your client is implicated in violating the *Lex Maiestatis*.

"I'm sure he has some explanation. I can't believe he is an assassin. I will find out what actually happened."

"Please do. The 5-day Notice of Trial was sent out yesterday, as you know. So I will see you before my Tribunal in 4 days, unless you have something to see me about sooner."

"Such as?"

"Such as a complete confession from Pudens. I want to know who he gave the snake to. Pudens himself seems guilty of treason and the sword of Damocles is suspended over his head. He might avoid the death penalty by telling the whole truth. If not, dire consequences will follow."

Casca rose from his seat. "It's a pleasure to appear before you again, *eminentissime*. I hope I will have more success this time than I did a few months ago."

"I'm sure your client will agree with that sentiment," responded the judge.

The same day Gaius Obesus, the assistant to the *munerarius*, appeared at the judge's chambers, escorted a little roughly by Vulso.

"My proposition is very simple, Obesus," began Severus as he was ushered into a seat across from the judge. "I know you bought an Egyptian cobra from the Marsic cult, brought it to Rome and then transferred the snake from the storeroom in the Flavian amphitheater to the defendant Publius Pudens, who left with it. I have witnesses who will testify to these events."

"I didn't know Pudens is a defendant. What is he charged with?"

"He is charged with treason under the *Lex Maiestatis* because that snake was put into the Emperor's bed in the Imperial villa at Lanuvium. We know that Pudens personally brought the snake to Lanuvium.

"Now, Obesus. I want you to be a witness for the prosecution, to testify that you personally gave the snake to Pudens in the basement of the amphitheater and that he himself took it away." Severus looked directly at Obesus. "Well?"

Obesus hesitated.

"I should add," continued Severus, "that if you do not agree to become a witness for the prosecution, you will become a defendant."

Obesus looked startled. "Me? A defendant? What did I do?"

"You bought the snake used in the assassination attempt and gave it to one of the assassins, namely Pudens. I thought I made that clear." Severus said this in a hostile tone of voice in contrast to the more pleasant tone his used when Obesus came in. "What do you want to be, Obesus? A witness for the prosecution or a defendant in a treason trial. One or the other. Which is it?"

Obesus took in what the judge said, his hostile versus his pleasant tone of voice, and replied without having to mull over all the implications. "In that case,

I agree to be a witness for the prosecution. I saw the cobra put into a wicker basket in the storeroom of the amphitheater and handed over to Pudens. He directed me to do it. I didn't know what the snake would be used for. My slave Nush was also a witness to the transfer of the snake to Pudens in the amphitheater."

"Fine. You will appear here in 4-days time, the day the trial of Pudens will begin. And one more thing, Obesus. Your slave Nush is no longer your slave. I have handed him over to become a slave of the Urban Cohort. I hope you will agree to sell him, *ex post facto*."

"What? I am to lose Nush? Why? I love him. I want him. No, I can't agree to this. He's mine. I bought him."

"I don't believe he wants you, Obesus. Your days of owning Nush are over. I can't force you to sell your slave, but I strongly advise you to do so. You will be compensated for his purchase price and you can buy some other beautiful boy. The slave stalls are full of them."

"But, but...."

"I want you to agree." Severus glared at him, with a menacing glare. His threatening look was unmistakable.

Obesus slunk into his chair. He looked depressed, driven down, as if he had no strength left. "All right," he said weakly. "All right. I agree."

"You've made the right decision. The legal documents for transfer of ownership of the slave Nush from you to the Urban Cohort are already drawn up and you can sign them on the way out. I'll see you in

4-days here in the Forum of Augustus for the trial of Pudens."

Obesus got up and passed into the anteroom where the court clerk Proculus presented him with documents for his signature and seal. The legal niceties having been taken care of, Obesus left, 'as fast as cooking asparagus', as the saying goes.

"Who's next?" Severus asked Vulso.

"Dendron," the secretary to Pudens. "I have him outside. I didn't bring along those six slaves Nush named. The ones with Greek letters for names. But I will, if you want them."

"No, I need to talk to Dendron first. Show him in."

Vulso went out and came back with a rather thin, almost emaciated looking, older man. He looked as thin as Pudens. His arms and legs and fingers looked like all bone, like sticks. The nickname 'tree' fit his appearance, in a demeaning sort of way. But despite his almost emaciated body, Dendron had a strong intelligent face. Severus thought his eyes seemed clever and disobedient. The judge motioned him to the chair across the table.

"Dendron, the reason I'm talking to you is…….."

"I know the reason, *eminentissime*. It's all over the house. Everyone knows the master is in serious trouble. He's being charged with treason and the trial is now in 4-days time." He smiled. "Whatever you want to know, *eminentissime*, I will tell you. You must know the saying, 'so many slaves, so many enemies.' Well, in our *familia* it's not just the slaves who hate the master, it's the freedmen, like me, who have serious problems with him as well. It's everyone actually.

He's a vicious, brutal man who insults and demeans everyone. He's a fanatic follower of Mithra and wants to spray bull blood over everyone. If you don't express reverence for Mithra, he will have you beaten. He's made everyone in the house become Mithra cult members, going through rites of initiation. I had to pass the rite of going over a ditch of water, blindfolded with my hands tied together with chicken entrails."

"Chicken entrails? That must have been unpleasant."

"Unpleasant? Disgusting is the word. Anyway, people in the house naturally return hate for hate, even if its's under their breaths, behind his back. So whatever I can do to help, I will be glad to do."

This is a nice development, thought Severus to himself.

"Well, then, Dendron. By the way, is that what you'd like me to call you? Or do you prefer some other name, perhaps your original name?"

"When the master called me Dendron to humiliate me, I hated the name. But now I've gotten to like it. I look like a tree, I know. But, you see, I like trees and am happy to be compared to one. Trees are beautiful, sturdy, long lasting. So, please, call me Dendron."

"All right Dendron. What I want to know first is about your recent trip to Lanuvium. When was it? How long were you there? Who was on the trip?"

"We started out on the first of this month, the Kalends. It took us most of the day to travel the 20 miles or so to Lanuvium. We spent four days at the Imperial villa and then it took us a day to return to Rome. So the trip lasted six days in all."

"I understand you and Pudens were in the lead *carpentum* while the slaves and luggage followed in another. Is that right?"

"Yes. There were six slaves in all, including Nush and the two *carpentum* drivers. They were also slaves of the household."

"What was the purpose of the trip?"

"The master said it was to visit his sister, who was staying at the Imperial villa in Lanuvium as a member of the Emperor's entourage."

"Did you meet her?"

"The master never introduced me to her personally, other than to say I was his private secretary. I was there for show, as were the six slaves."

"When did he meet her?"

"The first night. And also the next day, I know. In fact, I think they spent some time together on all 3 days we were there, mostly having meals together."

"Do you know if Pudens spent time with anyone else besides his sister?"

"I know he saw a doctor. I don't remember his name."

"Was it Posidippus?"

"Yes. That's the one. The master complained of various aches and pains and said he wanted a doctor to look him over. His sister sent him to that doctor."

"Did he meet anyone else?"

"Yes. Pudens always had a Mithraic text with him in both Persian and Greek. When he was told there was a Persian translator at the villa, he asked if the translator would look over the text and tell him if the Greek was a good rendition. I believe the translator discussed it with him during his time there and made some suggestions, for which Pudens expressed his thanks."

"Did your master talk with anyone else?"

"Let me think. No, there was no one else I know of. He did spend some time on a tour of the villa which was given to him by one of the *cubicularii*."

"Was the name of this *cubicularius* Eclectus, by any chance?"

"Yes. That's right. It was an informative tour, Pudens commented at some point. He said he even saw the Emperor's bedroom. And he and this Eclectus also had lunch together in the middle of the tour. I know that because I had a message his sister gave to me for him and I delivered it to him during lunch."

"Anyone else?"

"Not that I can recall."

"Not one of the Emperor's cavalry Praetorians, by any chance? His name is Lothar."

"Not that I know of."

"Anything else that happened there that you can tell me about?"

"Not that I know of."

"By the way, Dendron. There was a wicker basket on the top of the second *carpentum*, along with the luggage. Do you know what was in that basket?"

"I remember the wicker basket on top of the coach. I never knew what was in it."

"You say Pudens returned to Rome after 5 days. Did everyone who went with him, you, Nush and the rest of the slaves, also return with him to Rome?"

"Yes. We all went to Lanuvium together and re-turned together."

"Thank you, Dendron."

When the tree-like visitor left, Severus turned to Vulso. "They left Rome for Lanuvium on the first of the month, the Kalends he said, and spent four days there before returning to Rome. Six days in all. That means they left a day before the Nones, which this month falls on the 7th day. The Nones is the day the snake was put into the Emperor's bed."

"So Pudens must have delivered the snake to someone at the villa, who kept it hidden for a day before it was put into the Emperor's bed."

"Yes. So who did he deliver it to? Where was it kept?"

An hour later, Severus' former assessor, Gaius Sempronius Flaccus, came in.

"Gaius," began the judge, "would you be interested in becoming the prosecutor in a case coming before me. It's a treason case under the *Lex Maiestatis* and the defendant is a member of the Senatorial Order, Publius Plautius Pudens. The trial is set for 4-days from now."

"Will it be fun?"

"I think you'll like it. Also, the verdict is guar-anteed. Unless something unusual turns up, which I don't believe can happen, your prosecution will be successful. I will convict Pudens of treason."

"And the sentence?"

"I haven't decided on that yet. I may have to dis-cuss that with the Emperor. Any trial of a member of the Senatorial Order has political implications I'm not usually privy to. But I can virtually guarantee you will win the case."

"All right. I'm game. Give me the file and I'll look it over tonight and report back to you tomorrow."

Severus pointed to a pile of scrolls in one of the cubbyholes of the *scrinium*. As Flaccus began to pull them out and put them in a *capsa*, Severus asked him, "By the way, Gaius, what happened with your abortion case?"

"Oh, the woman changed her mind. She tried to cause a miscarriage by lifting heavy weights. That didn't work. Then she tried various potions recommended by doctors or friends, but they only made her sick. And she feels it's too dangerous to let doctors insert probes and pull out the fetus, piece by piece. Instead, she decided to have the child and if it survives childbirth, she will expose the baby."

"What does her husband say to that. Doesn't he object to exposing his child?"

"She told him it wasn't his child. He dropped his objection."

"I hope at least she will abandon it at the *Columna Lactaria*."

"The Milk Column. In the Forum Holitorium, the vegetable market. Yes, she intends to do that. That's where people commonly abandon babies, where they are often fed and cared for by kindly strangers. Also the baby might get lucky and be adopted, most likely as a slave, of course, but not always. Often people who want children but can't have them or have lost their own go to the Milk Column and adopt an abandoned infant."

"As we all know," said the judge, "this is a very uncertain world for children. The number who never make it through childhood is enormous. Even the Emperor has already lost four of his children to illness or disease."

Severus became grim, stoical and relieved at the same time. "Artemisia and I have been fortunate in that all three of our children have survived and are thriving. I don't believe in the gods, as you know, but if I did believe in any, it would be in the goddess Fortuna. In many ways, she has been watching over us." He then made the 'sign of the fig', the *manu fica*, with his hand curled into a fist, but with the thumb projecting out between the second and third fingers. It was a Roman sign to bring good luck and ward off evil. And although Severus was not particularly superstitious, with the children why take chances?.

The next day, having reviewed the file and grasped the nature of the prosecution and how he would present it, Flaccus agreed to become the prosecutor.

"A scoundrel. A traitor. A religious Mithra fanatic," he told the judge. "It would be a pleasure to present the prosecution's case against Pudens in court." Flaccus smiled broadly. "A real pleasure, especially since the verdict is already in."

XIX

THE TREASON TRIAL

The trial was set to begin at the 3rd hour. But unlike most trials in Rome, it would not be open to the public. No announcement had been posted in the Daily Acts on the newsboards in the Old Forum. Because the case concerned an attempt to assassinate the Emperor, and there was no political reason for exposing the plot and condemning the defendant in public, secrecy was appropriate. No one was supposed to plot to assassinate the Emperor; such plots were not supposed to exist. Accordingly, the trial of Publius Pudens would take place behind closed doors, inside the Praefectura building where the Court of the Urban Prefect was headquartered, rather than outside in the Forum of Augustus, where the Court of the Urban Prefect conducted most of its criminal cases.

But though the venue was different, the setup of the court was the same. The judge's Tribunal, a platform 4 feet off the ground, held the magistrate's chair, a camp chair with no arms or back. This was the same simple kind of chair used by magistrates in the old Republic and the practice continued under the Empire without change. Next to the judge on the Tribunal were his assessor and court clerk, who took down the proceedings in Tironian Notes shorthand, the popular shorthand invented by Cicero's private secretary Tiro. Since Severus' usual assessor Gaius Flaccus was to be the prosecutor, Severus asked Judge Memmius, the judge who had 'inherited' his chambers when Severus retired, to join him as assessor. Memmius was seated to Severus' right; court clerk Proculus to his left. Vulso, Straton and Alexander were seated below the Tribunal to the judge's right. Lictors, each carrying a bundle of rods as a symbol of judicial power, stood against the wall on each side of the Tribunal.

In front of the Tribunal were seats for the parties and their attorneys. Behind them were seats for the audience. In this case, the audience was composed only of a small sprinkling of court personnel. No random audience of passers-by, no court buffs, no lawyer's claques to cheer on or catcall one side or another.

At the 3rd hour, Severus mounted his seat on the Tribunal, clad in his formal judicial toga, bordered with its reddish-purple hem. He looked around in front of him. Flaccus, the prosecutor, was at one of the tables in front of the Tribunal. Casca, the defendant's lawyer, was at the other table in front of the Tribunal along with a young assistant.

But where was the defendant, Publius Pudens?

"I don't see your client at your table," said the judge to the defense lawyer. "It's the 3rd hour. Where is he?"

Casca shrugged his shoulders and splayed out his arms. "I don't know, *eminentissime*. He was supposed to be here. I expected him to be here. Perhaps he just got caught up in the morning traffic. Can we wait a few minutes?"

"I suppose so," said Severus, somewhat miffed as he got down from the Tribunal. "I'll be in chambers. If he's not here in a quarter of an hour, I will send lictors to his home to bring him here by force if necessary."

With that Severus went into the office behind, along with Judge Memmius, Alexander, Proculus, Vulso and Straton. The lawyers and lictors waited outside.

When a quarter of an hour had passed, Severus called the lictors into his chambers and started to give them instructions to go to the defendant's house, arrest him and bring him to the Tribunal. Just then a messenger came to the Tribunal and handed a message to Casca, the defendant's lawyer. Casca read it, motioned to the prosecutor Flaccus to come with him, and went to the door of the office behind the Tribunal and knocked. When it opened, he addressed the judge.

"*Eminentissime*, I have a message from the defendant's secretary Dendron. Publius Pudens will not be here for the trial. He is dead. He committed suicide early this morning."

Everyone looked at each other in silence.

Vulso made the first comment. "Good riddance."

No one contradicted the sentiment.

"The message also says," continued Casca, "that Pudens was visited yesterday by a group of senators, led by the Consul M. Aquilius Apollinaris. The Consul came to Pudens' home this morning and is now on his way here to explain to the *iudex selectus* what has occurred. He should be here shortly as he is on the way by litter."

Everyone settled down at a table. Court slaves brought wine, water and cups and a bowl of fruit. The wait was not too long. Within the hour the Consul showed up, was invited to the table and given refreshments.

Apollonaris had a drink of wine and looked at each person, one after the other. Then he spoke directly to Severus.

"Last night a group of senators, understanding the situation, visited Publius Pudens and in no uncertain terms told him to cooperate with the *iudex selectus*. He must name all his accomplices. We told him he would be convicted and unless he cooperated all his property forfeited, he would be sentenced to death and his name subjected to *damnatio*, excoriated forever. This would occur whether he was tried by the *iudex selectus*, as was imminent, or even if he, a member of the Senatorial Order, sought to have his case tried before the Senate or before the Emperor. His guilt was clear. His attempt to kill the Emperor was a national disgrace. But we assured him that the Emperor was a forgiving and merciful man, who would not seek vengeance."

"What did he say to that?"

"It was hard to tell. He was mostly scared, confused, blubbering. I don't think he could believe what was happening to him. But I thought I had given him a way out and I thought he understood he could save himself to some extent by cooperating.

"But this morning when I and two of the senators went back to Pudens' *domus* to escort him to court, we learned that instead of confessing and naming his accomplices, he had slit his wrists and settled into a bath of warm water, where he soon died."

"Did he at least leave a suicide note?"

"I regret to say he left no such writing."

"It's just as well," commented Severus, "because we wouldn't know whether any person he named was a real accomplice or not. Whatever Pudens might have said would be untrustworthy. On the other hand, we now know that our original assumption about people who were in both the entourages of Lucius Verus and Marcus Aurelius must be correct. One of the people who Dendron said Pudens met with when he visited his sister at the Imperial villa is most likely the person he gave the snake to and who put the cobra in the Emperor's bed. They are his sister Plautilla; the doctor Posidippus; the Persian translator Jangi; or the *cubicularius*.Eclectus.

"What about Lothar?" asked Straton, "the Praetorian cavalryman?"

"He is still a suspect. Pudens could have met with him unseen or he could be in cahoots with Plautilla. But in any event, we now must return to Lanuvium, to the Imperial villa, and continue the investigation. One of those suspects seems to be a conspirator, a Persian assassin."

"But they all seem so innocent," commented Alexander.

"Yes, they do," replied Severus, "but that just means that one of them is wearing a mask, like in the theater, where behind the mask of a god, will be a man. Behind the mask of Oedipus or Antigone or Achilles will be someone else. A Persian assassin could be behind the mask of someone quite different.

"How will you find out which one it is?" asked the Consul.

"We will question each of them. And one of them, the guilty one, will have to lie to us. So we will find the assassin by detection, *clarissime*. By detection."

XX

SEVERUS RETURNS TO LANUVIUM AND ONCE AGAIN QUESTIONS SUSPECTS

"What do you mean, *deliciae*," said Artemisia, "that the Persian assassin may be wearing a mask, appearing to be someone else?" She and her husband were sitting in their villa's garden, overlooking its swimming pool. The morning sun shone brightly and the sky was clear, but the weather was colder than the usual summer day. "Do you mean like the Persian translator who says he is Greek who lived in Persia as a boy might really be Persian who lived in Antioch as a boy?"

Severus looked up at the sun, walked over to the steps leading into the pool, took his left foot out of its sandal, and tested the water. "Still too cold. But yes, *deliciae*, what you just said is one possibility. But take the doctor Posidippus, for instance. What do we know about him? He may have studied medicine under Galen, as he alleges, but that may be to establish a disguise. Before that, where is he from? Who is he? And the *cubicularius,* Eclectus, what do we know about him before he was *cubicularius* to Lucius Verus? Where is he from? The current personality of any of the suspects may be a false mask. Even Plautilla. We know she was a Vestal, that's true, but she could use that to hide something else, some motive, some purpose we don't know about."

Just then, the children Flavia and Quintus rushed into the garden, followed by their black Molossian hound, Argos, his mouth wide open barking and his tail furiously wagging. The family orange and white Egyptian cat Phaon was already in the garden, hunched down in the surrounding foliage, with only his tail visible, stalking prey that no one else could see.

Quintus ran to the deep side of the pool, threw off his tunic and with a whoop dove straight in.

"Isn't it too cold?" asked Severus when the boy's head emerged above the water.

"Maybe for you, Tata, but not for me." He looked over at the dog. "Argos, c'mon in." Without any hesitation, Argos bounded into the pool and swam to the shallow side, where Flavia stood. She threw a stick into the middle of the pool. Both Argos and Quintus swam after it, but Argos snatched it up, swam to Flavia, dropped it at her feet and looked expectantly for another throw. She didn't disappoint him and threw the stick back into the pool. While Argos was chasing it down, Quintus climbed out and dried himself off with a towel from a table by poolside.

Just then Scorpus came out of the house to announce the *carpentum* was ready for the trip to the

Imperial villa at Lanuvium and that Vulso, Straton and Alexander were already aboard. Severus kissed his wife and children, had Scorpus help him put on his judicial toga, and boarded the *carpentum.*

The 5-mile ride downhill to Lanuvium took just under an hour. They were met at the villa's entrance by the *vilicus*, Epaphroditus, who had been informed by messenger the day before of the judge's coming visit. Epaphroditus had somehow overcome his grim worry about what had happened and resumed his public persona, showing smiles and excessive greetings when Severus descended from the coach.

"Everybody knows you want to speak to them today, *eminentissime,* and are on hand, except of course for Plautilla and Lothar."

"Except of course for Plautilla and Lothar? What do you mean by that?"

"But, *eminentissime*, we received your message the other day allowing Plautilla to leave the villa to attend the funeral of her brother and allowing Lothar to accompany her as a guard."

Severus was a little stunned. He had sent no such message. "Let me see the message."

Epaphroditus motioned to a slave who went into the villa while the *vilicus* escorted the judge and his aides inside. The slave returned with a small scroll and handed it to the *vilicus* who handed it to the judge.

"I never sent this message," said a miffed Severus. "It's a forgery." He handed the scroll to Vulso and asked Epaphroditus whether Plautilla said when she would return.

"No, she didn't."

"I'll need one of your villa's messengers to go to Rome. But first bring me a clean scroll for the message."

The scroll was brought and given to Alexander, who walked with Severus outside to take down the message in private.

"Marcus Flavius Severus, *iudex selectus* to Plautilla, greetings:

I understand your desire to attend your brother's funeral. I do not see that you had to forge a message from me instead of arranging it through me. I would have consented gladly. As it is, I expect you to return the day after the funeral, which should be tomorrow.
Seal / /."

"Have this sent to Publius Pudens' home on the Aventine Hill," he instructed his secretary. "That's where she should be found."

They went back into the villa, where Alexander gave the message to a messenger to take to Rome on horseback, while Severus and the others once again went into the spacious reading room of the Latin library where his interviews would take place.

"Send in the doctor Posidippus," said Severus to Epaphroditus. He then once again looked with admiration at the beautiful bronze statuary displayed in the room, while Alexander browsed red book tags hanging from scrolls in the cubbyhole shelves.

A few moments later the doctor entered and took a seat on the side of a table opposite Severus, Vulso, Straton and Alexander. He saw the fruit in a bowl and the wine and water already mixed and poured into glasses. The doctor ate a fig and took a sip of wine.

"What can I do for you this time?" asked the doctor, a little testily.

Severus didn't care for his attitude. "Doctor, what you can do is answer my questions, the first of which is that I understand you met with Publius Pudens here at the villa shortly after the Kalends of this month."

"Yes. That's so. He sought me out, complaining about this pain and that. Nothing serious, it seemed. I thought he was probably a hypochondriac."

"How long was your medical session with him?"

"I had to be polite and I took my time in answering his questions. It lasted about an hour."

"What did you tell him?"

"I told him that I could find nothing serious except that he looked pale and worn and was too thin. I told him that the school of Galen, which I follow, regards diet as the primary source of health and treatment, more than drugs or surgery or anything else. I told him a book Galen wrote called 'The Thinning Diet,' which I believe would be useful for him to follow."

"The Thinning Diet?" interrupted Severus. "If he were any thinner, he would be a skeleton."

"You do not understand, not being a doctor. The Thinning Diet would put his bodily humors in balance and make him healthier all over. We talked about the diet for a bit. I informed him that vegetables, especially eaten raw, fruit, seeds and lean meat are at the heart of the thinning diet, as is not cooking in too much olive oil. I touched on these subjects briefly, what is good to eat, what isn't, and recommended he get Galen's' writings and study them.

"When I finished, he left. Frankly I didn't think he heard a word I said, or if he did, he was not interested in following my advice. It would have been better to do so, I think, than committing suicide.

"So, may I ask you, judge, why did he commit suicide?"

"He was facing conviction on charges of treason. Suicide evidently seemed a better result than the consequences of a treason conviction. But there are a few other questions I'd like to ask you, doctor. The first is, where do you come from? How long have you been in Rome? How long have you studied with Galen? Tell me about your background."

"I can answer those quite quickly. I come from Berytus in the province of Syria, where I was born 42 years ago. My father was a doctor and I grew up studying medicine under him. When I heard that the famous doctor Galen was going to be at Rome, I decided to go there myself for two reasons. First, because I always wanted to study medicine under Galen and second because I always wanted to see Rome. And so I came here, and studied here for the four years he was teaching in Rome, starting 7 years ago. I hear he is coming back this year, and I will look forward to being his student again."

"Tell me this, Posidippus, does Galen discuss things in his lectures or writings such as poisons and snake bites?"

"Galen is encyclopedic. Of course, he discusses those topics, as well as many, many others."

"And are you familiar with Galen's discussion of snakebites?"

"To some degree. It's not my specialty, but yes, to some degree. I have to stop here, *eminentissime* to express my concern at the turn of this conversation." He became sullen. "Just why are you asking me about snake bites? I know of course that an Egyptian cobra was put in the Emperor's bed, but I had nothing to do with that at all."

"But Publius Pudens did. He was the person who brought the snake to this villa and gave it to someone, who then put it in the Emperor's bed. And you spent an hour with Pudens, as you just told me."

"I see. Well, it wasn't me he gave the snake to. Why don't you ask his sister about it? He saw her too, didn't he?"

"I will ask her."

"And you should also ask the *cubicularius* Eclectus about it. He was seen showing Pudens into the Emperor's bedroom, which he is not supposed to do."

"Who saw him?"

"One of the slaves, who told another slave, who told others, one of whom told me."

"I will ask him about it, you can be sure of that."

"Is there anything else, judge? Any charges you want to level against me? Any *vituperatio* against me you want to question me about? Any other nonsense you want to discuss?" The doctor was becoming angry, his face reddening.

"Control yourself, doctor. These questions are necessary to get to the bottom of what happened. If you did nothing, you have nothing to fear from me. If you conspired in the plot to kill the Emperor, you are doomed."

Severus made a motion of dismissal with his hand. Posidippus saw it and started to get up, but then stopped himself and sat back down.

"There's something I want to say to you, judge."

Severus nodded at him to say it.

The doctor gathered himself. "I resent being cooped up here in this villa, a prisoner. You probably have already interfered with my relationship with the Emperor, but I also have other patients in Rome I have to attend to." His manner was becoming surly and snide. "They need me. Your keeping me here therefore not only inconveniences me but works harm on my sick and needy patients."

"Is that all, doctor?"

"Yes."

"I will take that into consideration. You may go."

Posidippus got up and left, a scowl on his face.

The *cubicularius* Eclectus was the next suspect to come into the room for questioning.

"Eclectus," began the judge, "I hear you gave a tour of the villa to Publius Pudens, some weeks ago?"

"Yes. It was a courtesy to his sister Plautilla."

"How long did the tour take?"

"About an hour."

"Did you show him the Emperor's bedroom?"

"We passed by where it was, but I'm not allowed to bring anyone unauthorized into the *cubiculum*. So I didn't take him into the room. I only showed him the outside."

"Did he show any particular interest in any part of the tour?"

"I don't really remember. I just pointed out places, the libraries, the baths, the bedrooms, the guest houses, *et cetera* and he made acknowledging sounds. He didn't really ask any questions at all."

"Not even about the Emperor's bedroom when you didn't let him in?"

"Now that you mention it, it was about the only thing he did ask. He wanted to go in and see it, I said he couldn't and he asked me to describe it, which I did. Then we moved on."

"Tell me, Eclectus. Where are you from? How did you become *cubicularius* for the Emperor?"

"I was born a slave 30 years ago and as a child I was sold into the household of the Emperor Lucius Verus. I was raised there and worked under two other *cubicularii* and learned their jobs. I was later freed and become a *cubicularius* of Lucius Verus and when he died, I was transferred into the household of Marcus Aurelius. I think that was because Lucius Verus always spoke highly of me and of the job I did."

"One thing before you go, Eclectus. It was reported to me on good authority that you were seen showing Pudens into the Emperor's bedroom. Do you want to rethink what you just told me?"

Eclectus was stopped in his tracks. "Who says so? Tell me who says so?"

Severus stared straight into his eyes, his face grim. "I'm asking the questions Eclectus. Did you or did you not show Pudens into the Emperor's bedroom. Yes or no. If you lie to me, you are doomed."

Eclectus thought about it, trying to decide whether to deny it or come clean. His face was contorted. He even squirmed in his seat.

"All right, I admit it," he said at last. "Pudens gave me a gold aureus to show him into the Emperor's bedroom. I didn't see what harm it would do. He was a member of the Senatorial Order, after all, the brother of a Vestal, who is a member of the Emperor's entourage. So yes, I admit it. But who told you about it? I bet it was that doctor who was just in here. It was him, wasn't it? Well, you should ask him what he talked to Pudens about. They were overheard talking about snakes and snakebites."

"Who overheard them?"

"Slaves. They know everything that goes on in the villa. Yes, that doctor and Pudens must have been plotting together. Otherwise why all that talk about snakes and poisonous snakebites. Did the doctor tell you about that conversation? You don't have to answer. Of course he didn't."

"Tell me, Eclectus, when you showed Pudens into the Emperor's bedroom, did you unlock the door with a key you had with you?"

"Actually no. When the Emperor was in residence, he insisted his door not be locked. Only when he was not in residence was it locked. On the day of Pudens' visit, the Emperor was in residence. A few days later, when he had just left that afternoon, it also wasn't yet locked because it had to be cleaned first."

"So on that day anyone could have entered the bedroom that afternoon without a key. Is that right?"

"Anyone who was there, yes, I suppose so."

"Thank you Eclectus. You may go."

When he was dismissed, Vulso made a comment. "We seem to be getting somewhere. Everyone is implicating someone else in ways we didn't know about before."

"And not only that," added Straton. "Both of them lied to us. The doctor didn't tell us he talked to Pudens about snakes and snakebites. He mentioned only dieting. And Eclectus at first lied to us about showing Pudens into the Emperor's *cubiculum.*"

"So I wonder," added Alexander, "what the Persian translator Jangi has to say. Who will he implicate? Will he also lie to us?"

"Let's find out now," replied Severus and called for Jangi to be shown it. He took the seat on the opposite side of the table, had some wine and smiled at the judge and his aides.

"Jangi," began the judge, "I understand that earlier in the month you met with Publius Pudens when he was here visiting his sister. Is that so?"

"Yes. Briefly. He sought me out, saying his sister told him I was a Persian translator and would I translate something for him. I said 'of course' and he showed me a hymn to Mithra in Persian. I glanced it over and said my Latin was not good enough to translate this kind of poetry into Latin, but I could do it into Greek. He said that was fine. So that day I made a translation. It was a hymn about some of the Mithra nonsense they spout, about how the blood of the bull can cleanse the sins of man, *et cetera, et cetera.* Really idiotic stuff, if you ask me. But the next day I gave him my translation, he thanked me, and that was it. I never saw him again."

"How long did your talks with him last?"

"All together, not more than a half an hour, I would say."

"Is there anything else you can tell me about Pudens?"

"No. Just what I said. That's all there was to it."

"Do you have a copy of the translation you made, by any chance?"

"No. As I said, it's all nonsense to me. I made some notes on a wax tablet while I was translating, but erased it when I finished."

"Thank you, Jangi. You may go."

Jangi got up and left.

Severus had the doctor Posidippus recalled.

"Doctor, I have been told that you were overheard talking to Publius Pudens about snakebites. Is that true?"

Posidippus thought about it. "I'm trying to remember," he put on an act of trying to remember, his hand to his chin, his head looking up. Finally, he said, "it's possible. The man was a hypochondriac. He said he was afraid of mosquito bites, of spider bites, of snakebites, you name it. Dog bites, even. I tried to get rid of him. If you let hypochondriacs run on about their fears, they will never shut up. So I didn't pay much attention to everything he said, but yes he may have included snakebites in his list of fears."

"Thank you, doctor."

"May I ask, judge, when I can be let out of this place. I have a wife and two children in Rome and I want to attend the lectures of Galen which are about to start. I have a medical practice and patients to attend to in Rome. I've answered all your questions. Do I have to be confined further?"

Severus thought about it a few moments.

"No. Doctor, you don't. I'm going to let everyone go in a few days. You can all go back to Rome then, but I don't want you to go near the Emperor or even the Palatine. That will go for everyone else here, for Jangi, for Eclectus, for Plautilla and Lothar. Do you understand?"

"I do. I have no intention of going anywhere near the Emperor unless he asks to see me. If he does, you'll have to take it up with him."

"He won't ask you, I can guarantee it."

"Then I can get ready to go back to Rome. Goodbye."

Posidippus got up and left.

"Why are you letting them all go?" asked Vulso. "I thought we were confining them here until the case was solved."

"I don't believe there's anything more to be gotten from them here. Besides, I'm beginning to have an idea about who the person is that we're after."

"Who?" they all said at once.

"I'm not ready to say. I have no proof. I may be wrong. So let's keep it at that. Maybe each of you has a favorite suspect among our suspects, as well. At some point we will discuss it in depth. But for now, the investigation has to continue to gather facts. So call in Epaphroditus, the *vilicus*.

When Epaphroditus came into the room, Severus asked him, "how many slaves are there at this villa?"

"42."

"Please assemble them in an hour in a large room. I want to address them collectively."

Epaphroditus left.

"What's this all about," asked Straton.

"You'll see in an hour."

XXI

SEVERUS ASKS THE SLAVES
OF THE VILLA FOR HELP

An hour later, all the slaves of the villa were assembled in one room. There were men and women and children. All looked to be in good health and well taken care of. They were all dressed in good clothes and looked about as well as a group of slaves could look.

Severus went to the head of the room and addressed the group.

"I've been told that a few weeks ago, one or two of you or even more, I don't know, saw the *cubicularius* Eclectus show Publius Pudens into the bedroom of the Emperor. You may remember Pudens was the brother of Plautilla who visited her here.

"Also I've been told that a slave overheard part of a conversation between Pudens and the doctor Posidippus.

"I would like the slave who saw Pudens with Eclectus and the slave who heard Pudens with

Posidippus to come to me and talk to me about it. This is important and concerns the life of the Emperor. Any information you give me will be kept confidential and you will be amply rewarded for it. I will be in the Latin library where I have been interviewing people. Thank you."

Severus left and went back to the Latin library where he pleasurably browsed the scrolls, waiting for someone to show up. Bookstores and libraries were among his favorite places to be.

It wasn't long before a slave appeared at the door and was invited in. It was Cynthia, the cleaning slave who had found the cobra in the Emperor's bedroom. She left her wicker basket with cleaning implements and clothes and rags outside and hesitantly entered the room.

"I'm the one who saw Eclectus with Pudens," she announced.

"Tell me about it," said Severus.

"There's nothing much to tell. I was just passing in the corridor going from cleaning one room to another when I saw Eclectus and Pudens go into the Emperor's bedroom. They didn't even see me, their backs were to me."

"Do you know how long they stayed in the bedroom?"

"Not really. I went into another room to clean it. That's all I can tell you."

"That's enough. Thank you."

Severus handed her a gold *aureus* coin.

"Thank you, *eminentissime*. Thank you very much."

A short time later, another slave came to the door of the Latin library. "My name is Lysandra," she said. "I overheard the doctor and Pudens talking."

"Tell me about it,"

"I was cleaning the doctor's rooms and was in the backroom cleaning when I heard people come into the front room. I quickly finished up and went through the dividing curtain, excusing myself. The only thing I heard was the snatch of what they said before I came into the room. When I came in and they saw me, they became silent until I left. But before that, I heard them mentioning treatments for snakebites."

"Anything else. Did you hear, say, anything about spider bites or mosquito or dog bites?"

"Maybe someone said those things, I don't know. I heard the word 'snake,' that I know. And I heard the word 'treatment' and some medical words I didn't understand."

"Thank you, Lysandra. That is very helpful."

Severus gave her a gold *aureus*.

She thanked him profusely and left.

XXII

A LETTER FROM PLAUTILLA

Everyone was gathered at Severus' villa on Lake Nemi for a banquet and a discussion. Severus and Artemisia occupied the head couch in the *triclinium* dining room, while Vulso and Straton occupied another couch and Proculus and Alexander a third. Flavia and Quintus sat at a children's table in the same room.

The banquet followed the traditional Roman formula of beginning with an egg dish and ending with apples. The eggs were hard boiled in a sweet and sour honey vinegar sauce. The main course was Severus' favorite ostrich meat. "More tender, more succulent, more tasty than any other meat," he proclaimed while starting on his portion. The accompanying sauce was hot, sour, sweet and salty, with pepper, lovage, thyme, honey, mustard, vinegar, and salty *liquamen* in oil.

A patina of asparagus in coriander, wine and *liquamen* accompanied the main course.

When the apples came, along with figs, dates and grapes, everyone was full, satisfied and ready to talk about plans.

"I want to read you a letter from Plautilla.," began Severus. "You'll recall, of course, that she forged a letter from me allowing her and Lothar to leave the Imperial villa to attend her brother's funeral. I sent her a message that said I understood her desire to attend the funeral and if she had asked me I would have allowed her to go, but I didn't appreciate the forgery. I instructed her to her to return to the villa after the funeral. This is her reply. He unrolled a small scroll and read.:

"Plautilla Pudens, Vestal to Marcus Flavius Severus, *iudex selectus*, greetings:

"The reason I resorted to my own devices to attend my brother's funeral instead of asking your permission was simply because I wanted to take Lothar with me. You would have let me go, I'm sure, but not Lothar.

"I will return to the villa with Lothar, but in my own time. I do not fancy being a prisoner there. Instead, I'm going on vacation. You will not find me for a few weeks, so you don't have to look. Lothar with guard me, day and night.

"I understand from talk at my brother's house during the funeral that he committed suicide because he was facing a conviction for treason, having been the person who brought the Egyptian cobra to the Imperial villa.

"First, rest assured that he didn't give it to me. I hate snakes and wouldn't touch one, let alone know how to put it in someone's bed. I didn't know my brother very well at all. He was only 2 years old when I was 'captured' by the Vestals at age 7 to serve them. I only occasionally saw Publius at permitted family gatherings, but didn't ever really interact with him. Why he became a Mithra cult follower, why he sought to kill the Emperor, these are questions beyond me. I had nothing to do with any of it.

"Second, and most importantly, I don't believe my brother committed suicide. I believe he was murdered. Why? When I was at his funeral, he had first been placed on a couch at the foot of a small funeral pyre that was set up in a garden outside the funeral home. He was covered with a linen shroud instead of being displayed openly in the Roman tradition. I was told by the *libitinarius*, the funeral director, that he was told the corpse had to be covered according to Mithraic tradition. I had never heard of such a tradition and neither had the *libitinarius*, as he told me. He just followed instructions. I became suspicious and wanted to see my brother's face for myself. It might not even be my brother, for all I could see. So I made up a story that as a Vestal I had to perform a secret incantation over the body, with no one else present. I had Lothar usher everyone out of the garden. When everyone left, I pulled back the sheet and saw to my surprise that though it was my brother on the bier, his face did not show the calm, resigned, even content look of someone whose life seeped away in a warm bath, but his face was horribly contorted. Not only that, there was a bandage wrapped around his neck clotted with blood. I was able to pull the bandage back a bit and saw his throat was cut and then pulled it back some more to see that his throat was slit almost from ear to ear. Then I pulled back the shroud covering his wrists and saw they were intact, uncut. Now, can someone commit suicide by cutting his own throat in that way? Is it not apparent that he was murdered? I would also add that when I saw the state of the corpse I called Lothar and the funeral director back into the garden and showed them what I had discovered, so there are witnesses to what I saw. I now entrust the solution of the murder of my brother to you, *iudex selectus* Severus.

"Meanwhile, give my regards to your beautiful wife, Artemisia. Tell her I think of her constantly.

"*Vale*."

Severus let the scroll roll up. "What do you think of that?" he tossed out the question to everyone present.

"He was certainly murdered," began Vulso. "That's clear. And it's also clear that it was done to shut him up"

"Yes," added Artemisia, "he most likely was going to follow the advice of the Consul and senators to cooperate, to name his accomplices."

"So one of his accomplices at least was in his *domus*, where he must have been killed" added Alexander. "But who was it?"

"Who told us," asked Straton, "that Pudens cut his own wrists and died in the bathtub? That was a blatant lie. Whoever said that must be the killer, or one of them."

"Didn't we receive a message on the day the trial was supposed to begin that Pudens committed suicide?" recalled Proculus. "And wasn't that message from Pudens' secretary Dendron?"

"That's right," agreed Severus. "So therefore...."

Artemisia finished the sentence. "...therefore, Dendron could be a murderer. He must be one of the accomplices in the assassination attempt."

There was unanimous agreement.

Vulso and Straton got up simultaneously. They didn't have to be told to head to Rome and arrest Dendron for murder. But Severus motioned for them to sit back down.

"I want you to go after Dendron, yes, but we're not finished here. "I want to discuss our plans for the other suspects, who are still suspects. As you know, I've decided to let the doctor leave the villa. The *cubicularius* will stay there because it's his job to be there. The Persian translator can stay there as well. Any translations he is assigned can be done at the villa. And Plautilla and Lothar have already left.

"How will we keep track of the doctor," asked Artemisia. "How will we know what he's doing?"

"How will we know who he sees or who is seeing him?" added Vulso. "In other words, whoever is the Persian assassin who planted the snake in the Emperor's bed may still be planning and arranging an assassination, but how will we know it?"

"This is my idea," replied Severus. "First, Eclectus the *cubicularius* and Jangi are not going anywhere. They will remain at the villa under surveillance, with their incoming and outgoing messages and letters intercepted."

"Has that interception plan amounted to anything?" asked Vulso. "We've been intercepting all the messages from all the suspects for a while now. Has it turned up anything?"

"Not as far as I know," replied Severus. "The *curiosi* agents doing the interception seem to have learned nothing. There have been no incriminating messages. So either the suspects are deliberately not putting anything in writing, suspecting their letters are being intercepted, or they are sending incriminating messages, but in some kind of code or signals we are unaware of, or they may all be innocent. We just have to continue surveillance.

"Secondly, since Plautilla and Lothar are loose, we will have to find them and see what they're up to. I need a plan for that. Any ideas?"

No one had anything to offer.

"Well, then we may have to wait for them to reappear, as Plautilla says they will. When that will be, we don't know. But as for now, that leaves the doctor. He will be going to Rome both to return to his medical practice and to attend the forthcoming Galen lectures.

"How are we going to watch him all the time?" asked Alexander.

"My idea," replied Severus, "is this. It is traditional for guests when they leave an Imperial villa to receive a gift from the Emperor. I propose to have the Emperor bestow a gift on the doctor that will further our investigation."

"What kind of gift is that?" asked Proculus.

"A slave," replied Severus. "My idea is to give him a present of a slave who, unknown to him, will be our spy. A spy inserted into his household to report to us whatever he's up to."

"Won't the doctor be suspicious, especially if he is the Persian assassin?"

"Maybe. But so what. No one can refuse a present from the Emperor and the slave will be inserted into his home as our spy."

"Who will be the spy to be inserted into the doctor's household?" asked Straton.

"I don't know yet."

"I do," replied Straton.

"There is a slave of the Urban Cohort. He accompanied me on the trip to the Marsic cult and he is looking for a way to gain his freedom by helping us. He's already talked to me about how in our investigation of the return of Spartacus, we used a slave litter bearer as a spy to gain information and then freed him after the case was over. His name is Pectillus. He's clever and I think he could be a good spy for us."

"Talk to him about it," said Severus, "and make sure to warn him about the dangers of what he will be doing. If the doctor is the Persian assassin and suspects Pectillus is a spy, then Pectillus may end up murdered."

"I will make sure he is aware of the danger. But I think he'll want to take on the task of spying anyway."

"Then that's it. Our plans are underway. He nodded to Vulso and Straton, who took notice of his signal and arranged to head back to Rome to arrest Dendron for the murder of Publius Pudens.

SCROLL V

XXIII

DENDRON

Vulso and Straton showed up at the *domus* of the late Publius Pudens at the 2nd hour of the morning, leading a *contubernium* of eight soldiers of the Urban Cohort. Six took up positions surrounding the house, front, sides and back, while two accompanied Vulso and Straton as they knocked on the front door. When it was opened by a slave, Vulso and the others barged right in, asking to see Dendron. The slave backed off into the house, while telling the soldiers to wait just a minute. He would fetch Dendron. In less than a minute, Dendron was there, looking puzzled but with a helpful smile on his face.

"What can I do for you?" he said to Vulso.

"We'll go into a private room, if you don't mind," replied the centurion.

"This way," said Dendron as he led them into a side room off the atrium.

"Sit down," said Vulso, pointing to a seat on one side of a table. Dendron complied without question, while Vulso and Straton took seats on the other side and the two soldiers stood against the wall by the door.

"How can I help you?" asked Dendron again, but this time his tree-like body was visibly shaking like a leaf in response to Vulso's threatening tone of voice.

"Tell me, Dendron, how did Publius Pudens die?"

"He committed suicide."

"How did he do it?"

"He cut his wrists, settled into a warm bath and bled to death. I thought you knew this."

"Did you see any of this personally? Did you see Pudens cut his wrists? Did you see him in the bath?"

Dendron looked directly at Vulso. His voice and gaze were steady and seemingly honest. "Yes. I saw him commit suicide. I saw him slit his wrists with a knife he asked me to give him. Slaves drew a warm bath and I helped him settle into it, as he asked me to do. Why do you ask? Is there a problem?"

"Yes. There is a problem. We have information that Pudens did not die by suicide, by cutting his own wrists. We have good information that it wasn't Pudens' wrists that were cut, but his throat. He didn't commit suicide at all. He was murdered."

Dendron stood up. "An outrageous lie. Who said that?"

"Sit back down, Dendron. It's not your business to ask me questions. I'm asking you about the murder of Publius Pudens. And I want some honest answers, not more lies."

"I know who must have told you. It was that horrible sister of his, wasn't it? The former Vestal. I remember she had her big German brute usher us all away from the funeral pyre and she was there alone with the body. She made it all up. I don't know why. But you can ask any number of household slaves about what happened. Two of them drew the bath for Pudens. I'll call them and they'll tell you. What an outrage this accusation is. What a lie." Dendron was shaking again, whether in rage or in fear, it was impossible to tell. "She knows that the body has been cremated, so there is no way now to prove she's lying. But she is the liar here."

Vulso whispered something to Straton, who got up and left.

"I've just sent Straton to bring the funeral director, the *libitinarius*. His place is only a few streets from here, isn't it? We'll see what he has to say."

Dendron tried to stay calm, but then he began to fidget. He was recalling the day of the funeral. He remembered Plautilla being alone with the bier, but then he recalled she asked her German lover and the funeral director to join her. He looked at Vulso, who returned a confident, almost sinister smile.

They all waited in silence.

After about a quarter of an hour, Straton returned with a small, rotund man, with deep-set brown eyes, which shifted back and forth in a disconcerting manner. It was hard to look directly at him.

"Your name?" asked Vulso.

"I am Zeuxis son of Philemon."

"Did you conduct the funeral of Publius Pudens?"

"I did. My establishment is a few streets away. I was asked by that person sitting there, Dendron, to conduct the funeral."

"What did he tell you?"

"He said the Pudens had committed suicide and told me that the body was on a bier in the atrium, covered by a linen shroud. The shroud could not be removed. It was a practice of the cult of Mithra which Pudens observed and I was told it was at his request. Any removal of the shroud, Dendron said, would violate religious practice and be heretical."

"Did you look under the shroud?"

"No. I followed instructions and my workers brought the body to my funeral home for cremation outside in a pyre set up there. I told them not to lift the shroud, as instructed."

"Did there come a time when you actually were able to look under the shroud?"

"Yes. Just before the cremation was to take place, Pudens' sister, the Vestal, had me called from the funeral home. She was alone in the garden with the bier. She said she had to perform certain rituals for Vesta. Anyway, her German Praetorian called me into the garden where she had the shroud lifted off, exposing the body."

"What did you see?"

"I saw the corpse's throat had been cut and his wrists hadn't."

"Thank you. You may wait outside."

Vulso looked at Dendron.

"What do you have to say now?"

Dendron slumped over in his chair, his head in his hands. He then looked up.

"He's lying. The sister paid him off. Pudens committed suicide by slitting his wrists, just as I said. I'm telling the truth. The sister and the funeral director are lying."

"You're under arrest, Dendron."

Vulso motioned to one of the guards standing by the door. He went to Dendron, stood him up, pulled his hands behind his back, and snapped handcuffs on him.

"We'll take him to see the judge," said Vulso. "You'd better think things over on the way, Dendron. Because if you stick to your lying story, you're finished."

Dendron said nothing as he was taken out of the *domus* and led along the streets by accompanying soldiers, has head hanging down, his face sad and dejected, his pace slow and trudging, but responding to periodic shoves from behind. He was a sorry sight, as was noticed by the gathering morning crowds filling the streets, hurrying this way and that. "Another victim for the lions," said some. "He doesn't have enough meat on him for even a lion cub," noticed others. "Poor soul," commiserated more than a few.

By the time Dendron reached the Forum of Augustus and was taken to see Judge Severus in his chambers, the prisoner appeared to be a broken man. And Severus was ready for him because Vulso had already briefed him on what had occurred, having walked briskly far faster ahead of Dendron and his escort. The table in chambers was set with wine and fruit, which Severus offered to the prisoner as he was pushed into a chair across from the judge.

"Take your time, Dendron. Have some wine. Refresh yourself. But understand that we believe

Pudens was murdered. So I want you to tell me everything. If you're truthful and honest, things will go easier for you than if you're not. You know, as a Roman judge, I have discretionary powers, particularly in sentencing. I can sentence someone to a fine, to beatings, to exile, to death. Whatever is appropriate. I hope you will choose to help me with correct information and to help yourself with a more lenient punishment."

"I will help you, *eminentissime*. I will tell you the whole truth."

"That's the wisest course." Severus leaned back in his chair. "I'm listening."

Dendron began to spin out the story of his life. "I was born a slave about 60 years ago, I'm not certain exactly, because unlike most free citizens my birth was not registered. I was born in the reign of Trajan, in Florentia, a slave in the household of Manlius Aquilius Macrinus, a descendant of an old Etruscan family and a member of the Senatorial Order. Because I had red hair, I was called Rufus. As a slave born into the *familia*, I was treated more or less as a family member, respected if not loved. My mother died in childbirth and my father died when I was 5 years old. They were both actually slaves not of Macrinus, but of his wife Camilla, and I was therefore her slave. She had me given a certain education, and I was taught to read and write and count. Since I was good at these subjects, I performed scribal and secretarial duties for Camilla as I grew up."

Severus, Vulso and Straton listened attentively, though Vulso was starting to wonder when Dendron would get to the point, the murder of Pudens.

"When Camilla's daughter Aquilia reached the age of 15, a marriage was arranged with Publius Pudens, who was then in his 20's. I was given to Aquilia as a wedding present and became her scribe and secretary in the Pudens' *familia* in Rome. Soon after the marriage Aquilia became pregnant and had a child who died in infancy. This happened two more times, and on the third she died in childbirth, as did the child. I was freed in her will and automatically became a Roman citizen. I stayed on in the Pudens' household as his secretary and scribe."

"Very interesting," interjected Severus. "But now get to recent events. Tell me about the death of Pudens. Why did he want to kill the Emperor?"

"For Mithra."

"What do you mean for Mithra?" asked Vulso. "Mithras is a popular god in the Roman army and professes loyalty to the Emperor as one of their main principles."

"Yes," responded Dendron. "That is the Roman form of Mithraism. Romans call the god Mithras, instead of Mithra, the Persian name. Pudens was a fanatical worshipper of the Persian Mithra. Loyalty to Persia, to Parthia, to Iran is their principle, besides, of course, of all the *nugax* of Mithra worship, the bull's blood, the grottoes, *et cetera.*"

"Where and when did he become a Mithra fanatic," asked Severus.

"I don't know exactly. He used to say when he was in the East years ago, when he was on the staff of some legion. He used to say the legions worshipped the wrong Mithra. He worshipped the right one. Not the Roman Mithras, but the Persian Mithra."

"Did he decide to kill the Emperor then all by himself? Was it his idea?"

"I don't think so. But I know he agreed with the idea. He was incensed by the sacking of Ctesiphon by the Roman army and the destruction of Mithra temples there. He said that it was ordered by both Lucius Verus and Marcus Aurelius and that Mithra would see that they pay for it. Also, you have to understand that he was an embittered and resentful person. He had lost three children to diseases and his wife died in childbirth. He said the Roman and Greek gods were ineffective and false. He hated them. Mithra, the Persian god, had become his savior."

"You just said you don't think it was his idea. So whose idea was it? Was he ordered to do it?"

"I don't know for sure. But once he said to me, this was when he had already decided to commit suicide, he said a lion ordered him to do it. He laughed, as if he were making a joke. The lion, he said, put a snake to sleep and was now putting him to sleep. I'm not sure what he meant. I know that in the *Mithraeum* in our *domus*, like in all *Mithraea* there is a scene in front of Mithra slaying the bull. And on the wall behind it, as in many *Mithraea,* there is a statue of a fire-breathing Mithraic god with wings, a lion's head and a snake coiled around its body. Maybe he meant that lion and that snake. But also I know that the lion is one of those Mithraic ranks, so maybe the person who ordered him to kill himself, who also put the snake in the bed, was a Mithra

follower with the rank of Lion. Maybe he was referring to that. I don't know."

"Who was the person at the villa Pudens gave the
snake to? Who was that Lion you're speaking about?"

"I have no idea. What I told you before about the
trip was all I know. We, that is Pudens, myself, and
the slaves, left on the Kalends, were away for 6 days,
and all returned to Rome the day before the Nones."

"Now, Dendron, tell me why you murdered
Pudens?"

"Me? Murder? I didn't murder him. He committed suicide. I didn't tell the truth about the manner of
his suicide because he told me what to say. You see,
he didn't want to die like a Roman by slitting his own
wrists and die in a warm bath, like Seneca for instance.
He wanted to die in a Mithraic way, slain like the sac-
rificial bull that is depicted in every Mithraeum, by
being stabbed in the neck and having his throat slit.
He wanted his blood to flow out like the blood of the
Mithraic bull which they believe will fertilize the world,
which they pour out onto every initiate. So Pudens
asked me to cut his throat for him like Mithra, but to
say he cut his own wrists like a Roman because I would
get in trouble if it became known how I helped him die.
He also told me to cover his corpse with a shroud so no
one would know the real way he died. So yes, I stabbed
him in the neck and then cut his throat. But no, it was
not murder. He ordered me to do it. To help him commit suicide, like someone holding a sword for a Roman
to fall on. Like Brutus did, for instance."

Dendron sat back with a somewhat satisfied look
on his face, with even a hint of a smile. Severus, Vulso

and Straton all looked at him with a skeptical look on their faces. No one believed a word of what he was saying about the demise of Pudens.

Severus had a scowl on his face. "Dendron, I don't believe the story you just told me about the death of Pudens. I think you murdered him to keep him from revealing the names of his accomplices in the plot to kill the Emperor. That's what I think."

"But what I said is the truth, I didn't..."

"Shut up. I don't believe you. Vulso, put him in a holding cell in this building and we will decide what to do next."

"Torture him, I say," said Vulso looking directly at Dendron. "He's a liar and torture will bring out the truth."

"No," exclaimed Dendron looking frantically back and forth at Severus and Vulso. "No. I'm a Roman citizen. You can't torture me."

"Ordinarily that would be correct, Dendron," informed the judge calmly. "But attempting to murder the Emperor is a treason case, and citizens can be tortured in pursuit of the truth in treason cases."

"But you are accusing me of murdering Pudens. That can't be, that is not treason." He looked as if he was inventing an argument on the spot, pulling it out of thin air. "In fact, if Pudens himself committed treason by attempting to murder the Emperor, even if I did murder him, which I deny, because he committed suicide, even if I did murder him, I should be given a medal for killing a traitor. I should be given the Civic Crown for saving the life of a citizen, for saving the life of the Emperor."

"Take him to the holding cell, Vulso," said Severus in response. "Dendron, it's a clever argument, but I don't buy it. There will be no medal coming to you. That's certain. Right now, I think you murdered Pudens to shut him up, to keep him from revealing his accomplices in plotting to kill the Emperor. That makes you an accomplice in a treason case. So if you don't tell me the truth, I will order judicial torture for you tomorrow morning. Think that over."

He nodded to Vulso, who then dragged Dendron out of his chair and out of the room.

"He's quite a lawyer," commented Straton. "He pictures himself as a patriot for murdering Pudens."

"Yes. It's a clever argument, isn't it? And he's quite a clever person. We must keep that in mind when assessing what he's told us. He's knows things he is not telling us. What they are and why he's not talking are what we have to find out. That story about the Mithra Lion ordering Pudens to kill himself. Did Dendron make that up? Or did it really happen. I don't know. Maybe he may clarify things under torture. Maybe that will work, maybe not. We'll see to-morrow morning."

Severus called his court clerk into the room. "Quintus, arrange for the *quaestionarius* to be here tomorrow morning at the 3rd hour. And set up the Tribunal in the torture chamber, so everything will be legal."

Proculus shivered at the thought.

So did Severus.

XXIV

IN THE COURTROOM FOR JUDICIAL TORTURE

The *quaestionarius* was a big, brutal looking man, with an evil glint in his eyes and on his face. It was part of his job to look like that. The night before the torture was scheduled, he visited Dendron in the holding cell to look him over, to decide what torture instrument would be most effective. He handled Dendron like a piece of meat, pulling his arms and body this way and that, not caring whether he hurt him by the rough inspection or not. Dendron suffered through it, trying to draw on what he knew of Roman Stoicism, but nevertheless he was scared and shaking.

"Pleasant dreams," said the *quaestionarius* as he left. "I'll see you in the morning."

Dendron had no dreams that night because he couldn't sleep at all. By the time he was dragged into the torture chamber by two court lictors he was an exhausted, frightened, beaten man. He was placed in front of the Tribunal set up for the occasion. He saw the judge seated on his magistrate's chair on the 4-foot high platform, dressed in his magistrate's toga.   Flaccus, his assessor, Proculus, the court clerk, and Vulso and Straton were also seated on the Tribunal on either side of the judge. Dendron also must have seen the statue of Jupiter Fidius, the god of good faith, which made the place into an official courtroom. By a slight turn of his head, he could also see the *quaestionarius* standing next to a horrible torture mechanism. Dendron recognized it as *fidiculae,* a collection of ropes used to pull the bones of out their sockets and dislocate joints. Dendron, like most Romans, knew what it was because he had seen it in operation before. In Rome most judicial torture, like executions, were carried out in public so the populace would know the government was doing its utmost to catch and punish criminals and keep order in society.

Dendron looked at the torture instrument, at the *quaestionarius* and at the judge on the Tribunal.

"I'll confess everything," he said to the judge. He was again shaking like a leaf. "There is no need for torture. I'll confess everything."

"I'm listening," replied Severus. "Tell me everything."

Dendron took a deep breath and looked up at the judge.

"It was the *spasaka*," he said. "Pudens called it the Persian secret service. The 'eye' of the Great King, it was called. Like our *curiosi*, only older and much better, he said. The *spasaka*. They ordered him to kill the Emperor. They ordered him to commit suicide."

"How do you know this?"

"Pudens told me so. He told me that's why he attempted to kill the Emperor. He told me before his death that the *spasaka* ordered him to commit suicide so he would be unable to name confederates. I'm not sure why he told me all these things, but he was about to kill himself, so maybe it was a last act to clear his conscience, a dying catharsis. I can't say. But he swore me to secrecy. He said the *spasaka* would kill me if I ever told anyone what he was telling me."

"How did the *spasaka* tell him these things? Who told Pudens what the *spasaka* wanted?"

"I don't know that. I swear by all the gods. He never told me who was his contact from the *spasaka*. I swear. I would tell you if I knew. But he never told me."

"Even if he didn't tell you, maybe you know anyway. It was only in the few days leading up to the trial that the *spasaka* must have told him to kill himself. Who visited him during those days?"

"No one except a delegation of senators and a Consul the day before. But he did leave the house on the day after he received the 5-day notice of trial. He was out all afternoon. That night he received a message. I don't know what it said, but after that he began to prepare for his own death. The next day he made out a will and told me that he wanted to die by being stabbed in the neck and having his throat cut, like the Mithraic bull. He wanted to do it on the night before the trial. And he wanted me to do it. I objected, but he said no one was to know. I wouldn't get in any trouble because I was to say he committed suicide by slitting his own wrists and dying in a warm bath. It is in his will that I am to receive a bequest for helping him commit suicide in the Mithraic way. He sent the will to his sister in Lanuvium. Not only is she his sister, but she's a Vestal and one of the traditional functions of the Vestals is to be caretakers of wills. His slave Epsilon delivered the will to her there the day before Pudens' death. If you want to see that will, ask Plautilla for it. It will show that he ordered me to kill him as a Mithraic way of committing suicide."

"Who delivered the message to Pudens to kill himself?"

"It was just a messenger. I don't know who sent it. It was written on a small wax tablet, that I know. I don't know if he erased the message, but if he didn't the message may still be among his effects in the *domus*."

"As for the will, unfortunately, I don't know where Plautilla is. She's not in Lanuvium and…"

"I know where she is. At the funeral she told me where she would be in case I had to contact her. She's at Antium. Only about 30 miles from Rome. The Pudens family has a villa there for summer vacations, not far from the villa of Nero. The slave Epsilon can take you there. He's been to the villa many times."

"You said Pudens swore you to secrecy. He threatened that if you told anyone the *spasaka* would kill you. So why are you telling us?"

Dendron looked at the judge. Then looked at the *quaestionarius* and the torture device, and then back at the judge. "Torture is worse than death."

"One other question, Dendron. When Pudens left his house the day after receiving the 5-day notice of trial, did he have someone with him? A slave, perhaps?"

"No. He was alone."

"How was he dressed?"

"As usual. He always followed the protocol for members of the Senatorial Order to appear in public only in togas, with the broad stripe on his tunic visible. He was dressed as a senator."

"That's all for now, Dendron. Torture is postponed while we check out what you have told us."

Severus told two lictors to take Dendron back to his holding cell. "Vulso and Straton, I don't have to tell you to go immediately to Pudens' domus and one, search it for that wax tablet from the *spasaka* and two, bring back the slave Epsilon."

A few hours later Vulso and Straton returned to the Forum of Augustus from Pudens' home on the Aventine Hill. They brought with them a small wax tablet and the slave Epsilon.

"Here's the tablet," said Straton as he handed it to the judge. "Read it."

Severus opened the threads and the tablet. The message on it was succinct, but instructive. It was written in Greek and said simply, "Lion to Soldier. Kill yourself."

"Lion to Soldier?"

"Those are ranks in Mithraism," informed Vulso. "One starts as a Raven, then becomes a Bride, then a Soldier, then a Lion *et cetera*. This was an order from Pudens' superior in Mithraism."

Epsilon was brought in and questioned about Pudens' villa, where it was and could he take Vulso there.

"Certainly I can, *eminentissime*. The villa is just outside Antium. It's a small villa with six Doric columns in front and a green tiled roof."

"By the way, Epsilon, I gather you went on the trip to the Imperial villa at Lanuvium with your master and other members of his *familia*?"

"That's right, *eminentissime*. It lasted about six days or so. I was there along with other slaves, Delta, Mu, Rho, Iota, Kappa and Nush. Iota and Kappa were the *carpentum* drivers. Nush was no longer Pudens' slave, but he was on loan from his new master Obesus. That's what I understood.

"What did you do there?"

"Run errands. Basically nothing. All the slaves were there for show. We all returned together. I was in the second *carpentum* with Delta, Mu and Rho. The master, Dendron and Nush were in the first *carpentum*."

Epsilon was told to wait outside and Vulso would tell him what to do.

"I have to see that will. Vulso, you go to Antium with Epsilon. And tell Plautilla I want to see her here. Bring her back with you if you can. Tell her I have a number of questions for her that can't wait. Tell her to come voluntarily or I will be compelled to bring her back by force. Have the local *Vigiles* watch her villa in case she tries to escape to a new hiding place and tell her she is being watched. But in any case, bring Pudens' will. As a magistrate I have the legal right to see it."

Vulso left. It should take two days to complete his mission. Meanwhile Severus would turn his attention to what was happening, if anything, with Posidippus, the doctor. Had the spy they placed in his house found out anything? He told Straton to check into that immediately. And with that, Severus headed to the gymnasium in the nearby Baths of Trajan to practice throwing his javelin. It would help him think.

XXV

STRATON MEETS PECTILLUS
AT A BOOKSTORE

At the 9th hour of the next day, Straton sauntered into Caelius' bookstore on the Vicus Sandalarius. This was not only Judge Severus' favorite bookstore in the whole City, but he and Caelius were personal friends and the bookstore was often used as a place for message drops or clandestine meetings in cases the judge was working on. This day, that was the purpose of Straton's visit.

"He's in the back," said Caelius, looking up from a book he was reading, as Straton came in. "In the Greek music section."

Straton nodded and wove his way along corridors into the back section where Pectillus was waiting. The meeting had been prearranged through signals agreed upon when Pectillus was recruited to spy on Posidippus, the doctor. The signals were simple; bringing off the meeting was not so simple. Pectillus was inserted into the doctor's house, an apartment on the second floor of an *insula* on the Esquiline Hill. Straton had arranged with a resident on the second floor of an apartment across the street to display a flower pot on his balcony whenever Straton asked him to. The flower pot was a signal to Pectillus across the way that Straton wanted to meet him that day in Caelius' bookstore at the 9th hour, if possible. If not, Straton would be at the bookstore every day at the 9th hour until they met or until the flower pot was removed. The owner of the flower pot, an old woman, received a nice sum of money for her cooperation and didn't know or care what the pot was for.

"There you are," said Straton as he came upon Pectillus seated in a chair reading a scroll.

"Aristoxenus on music theory," said Pectillus, holding up a scroll. "Pretty interesting, actually. He quotes Plato as saying 'musical innovation is full of danger to the State, for when the modes of music change, the fundamental laws of the State change with them.' Do you think this is true?"

"I don't quarrel with Plato," replied Straton. "A very, very wise and insightful philosopher. And he must have observed what went on in the numerous City-States of his day. The music of Sparta was in the Dorian mode, militaristic, and Sparta was a militaristic State. Other City-States where lascivious music was favored probably courted pleasure above all. So he probably knows what he's talking about."

Pectillus furled the scroll and put it back into a cubby hold behind him. "I hope we won't take too long. I had a hard time getting away and I have to be back soon."

"Then report to me now. What's been happening. Does he accept you?"

"Does he? You would be surprised. I'm a present from the Emperor, so he thinks. I was a slave who was part of the Emperor's entourage, so he thinks. I know people, slaves, freedmen, administrators, *et cetera*, who work for and with the Emperor, so he thinks. And that's just dandy for him, so he says."

"What do you mean?"

"The doctor is miffed beyond words at what has happened to him. There he was, one day an intimate of the Emperor, one of the chief physicians the Emperor relied on, and the next day he is not allowed to see the Emperor at all. And he blames your judge, the *iudex selectus* Marcus Severus for his downfall. All he can talk about, all he prays for, is that Judge Severus gets sick and has to come to him for treatment. 'I'll bleed him so he'll never forget it,' says the doctor. 'Oh, how I'll bleed him.'"

"I'll warn the judge," responded Straton, laughing. "Though I don't think Judge Severus has it in mind to seek out Posidippus as his doctor if he got sick. But tell me about you. How are you getting along?"

"Fine. Just fine. Posidippus, as I said, thinks that I have influence with people close to the Emperor. So he's treating me very well. He says he wants to make me into one of his assistants and is teaching me medicine. He takes me on visits to patients, he brings me in to watch him treat patients in his office. He's even going to take me to a lecture by Galen in a few days. I'm reading one of Galen's books now. Posidippus recommended it and lent it to me from his library. I'm actually finding this whole thing very interesting."

"That's all good. You must be gaining his confidence. But has he done anything suspicious, in the way we talked about? Is there anything of a Persian nature you've seen?"

"When he prays that your judge gets sick and has to see him for treatment, he prays to the Persian god Mithra. But then he also prays to Jupiter, to Zeus, to the god of the Jews, to the god of the Christians, to Marduk, the Babylonian god, to any god he can think of. So I don't think that's too important.

"But there is one thing that might interest you. And that happened yesterday. I went with him to a Temple of Mithra and he left me outside for about an hour. He said he went to treat a sick priest in the temple and that I wasn't allowed in because I was not an initiate of the Mithra mystery cult. He said he was, but he said he was only a Raven, whatever that means."

"It's the beginning rank in Mithraism. I'll report this to the judge. Good work. Keep at it."

Pectillus got up and left to return to the doctor's apartment. Straton waited a while and then left to head back to Judge Severus' chambers.

XXVI

THE *CURIOSI* REPORT ON THE SUSPECTS AT LANUVIUM

When Straton reported back to Judge Severus, telling him what Pectillus said, Severus started to laugh. "If he thinks I'll ever go to him if I'm sick, Posidippus has another thing coming. I wouldn't go to him before I heard Pectillus' report. Now, well, now it's even more impossible. Bleed me, will he? I'm more likely to draw his blood figuratively, than he is to draw mine literally.

"Anyway, Straton, while you were gone, I received a message from Brennus of the *curiosi*. You'll remember there's still a surveillance of the suspects remaining at the Imperial villa at Lanuvium, the Persian translator Jangi and the *cubicularius* Eclectus."

"I remember. The *curiosi* agent at the villa was to intercept all incoming and outgoing messages to or from the suspects, read and copy them, and deliver them if advisable."

"Correct. And they also were to interrogate the messengers who arrived with messages and use *curiosi* agents to deliver outgoing messages. So, they did all that, and Brennus has passed along copies of three new intercepts to me." Severus pointed to a small pile of scrolls on his desk.

"What do they say?"

"I just got them. So call in Proculus and we'll read their mail together."

When Proculus came in, Severus told him what the letters on his desk were.

"They all concern Jangi the Persian translator. There was no mail in or out to or from Eclectus."

The three then randomly took one scroll from the pile and began to read.

"Nothing," said Proculus. "Just a letter to a woman, apparently his concubine in Rome."

"And this one," said Straton, "is to someone in the government bureau for Greek correspondence '*ab epistulis Graecis,*' about a problem in a petition."

"And the one I have," said Severus, "is also about government business. Of course, these could be in code, but I don't think so. So far we have nothing against either Jangi or Eclectus. It may be that they are innocent of attempting to kill the Emperor, that neither of them is the Persian assassin we're looking for."

"Why do you say that?" asked Straton and Proculus almost simultaneously. "Just because we lack evidence as yet?"

"Not just that. It's also because now I think I know who the assassin is. But I can't be certain until I see Pudens' will. So until Vulso gets back with it, I'll have to hold off. I've been made a fool of, I think. But that's over. Now it's my turn to strike."

SCROLL VI

XXVII

VULSO RETURNS FROM ANTIUM WITH THE WILL OF PUDENS

It was two days after Vulso and Epsilon left for Antium that they returned. At about the 9th hour, mid-afternoon, Vulso walked into Judge Severus' chambers with a smile on his face.

"Vulso," exclaimed Proculus, "the judge will be glad you're back. He's at the throwing field at the Baths of Trajan throwing his javelin. I'll send a messenger to get him."

Proculus walked into another room in the colonnade where court slaves were always waiting, and told one of them to run to the Baths and tell the judge that Vulso has returned. The slave left immediately, running.

Other court slaves brought wine and fruit for Vulso, who waited in the judge's chambers for Severus to return. It wasn't long before he did.

"Vulso, I'm glad you're back. How did it go? Did you get the will? Did you bring back Plautilla and Lothar?"

"I have the will with me. Plautilla promised that she and Lothar will be back tomorrow. She said she will be staying at Pudens' *domus* on the Aventine."

"Good work. Let me see the will."

Vulso rummaged in the musette bag he had with him and pulled out a scroll. "Here it is," he said as he handed it to the judge.

Severus inspected the seal on the scroll, saw it was Pudens' seal, and then broke it, unfurled the scroll and began reading.

After a few minutes, the judge let the scroll furl back. "That's it, then. If this is authentic, I know who the Persian assassin must be. But first we must make sure. So Vulso, go to Pudens' *domus* and find examples of his handwriting. Ask the slaves to find them for you. Also find examples of his secretary Dendron's handwriting. We will compare these examples with the writing in the will."

"What's in the will? Who is the assassin?"

Severus didn't answer those questions directly. Instead he issued instructions to Proculus.

"Quintus, send a messenger to the Imperial villa at Lanuvium and have Jangi and Eclectus brought back here.

"Also send a messenger to Brennus at *curiosi* headquarters and tell him to be here in my chambers in two days at the 3rd day hour. Suggest to him that he bring a few large agents with him.

"Then send a message to Posidippus, ordering the doctor to be here at that same time.

"Send another tomorrow to the Pudens house on the Aventine. Telling Plautilla and Lothar to be here the next day at the 3rd hour. Also have the slave Epsilon brought here as well.

"Then send a third messenger to have Obesus the *munerarius* from the Flavian amphitheater and Nush at the Castra Praetoria be here at the same time.

"Have Dendron brought from his holding cell to be at the gathering.

"I will tell Artemisia and Alexander and Straton."

"You're bringing everyone here, all the suspects, everyone with relevant information, everyone interested, everyone involved. Am I right in assuming you will have an important announcement to make?" Vulso concluded with a knowing smile.

"Yes. I will expose the Persian assassin. I will tell you who put the snake in the Emperor's bed. I will tell you who ordered Pudens to kill himself. In short, I will solve the case."

XXVIII

JUDGE SEVERUS EXPOSES
THE PERSIAN ASSASSIN

The Tribunal was set up in the largest room inside the colonnade of the Forum of Augustus. Judge Severus sat on the magistrate's camp chair in the middle of the 4-foot platform, with his assessor Flaccus on his right and on his left, his court clerk Proculus taking down the proceedings verbatim in Tironian Notes. In front of the Tribunal was the corona, a semi-circular area of benches for the courtroom witnesses and audience. Facing the corona, but below the Tribunal, were Vulso, Straton and the *curiosi* officer Brennus on the judge's right. To his left were Artemisia and Alexander.

Seated in the first row of the corona were the five suspects from the Imperial villa at Lanuvium, from the judge's left to right, Posidippus, the doctor; Jangi, the Persian translator; Plautilla, the Vestal; Lothar, the Praetorian; and Eclectus, the *cubicularius*.

In the second row behind them were four other persons relevant to the investigation. From left to right, Obesus the *munerarius* at the Flavian amphitheater; Nush, the Persian slave first of Pudens, then of Obesus, now of the Urban Cohort; Dendron, the freedman and secretary of the deceased Publius Pudens; and Epsilon, the slave of Pudens.

To one side of the Tribunal was the statue of Jupiter Fidius, necessary for turning the setting into an official court. Standing against the wall behind and to the sides of the Tribunal were four lictors, each with his *fasces*, the bundle of rods symbolic of judicial authority. The ax which usually was in the center of the *fasces* was by tradition removed inside the city of Rome. Also against the wall in back of the corona were four large, tough looking *curiosi* agents which Brennus had brought with him at the suggestion of the judge.

Judge Severus surveyed the scene, deliberately pausing to look at each person in the corona one by one. In the front row, he saw the doctor looking at him with hostility, while the Persian translator and the *cubicularius* showed no emotion at all. Plautilla looked interested, but stole furtive glances at Artemisia, while Lothar, her Praetorian paramour, looked stolid and dull. In the second row Severus saw Nush smiling at him, almost with reverence, and Obesus looking nervous and wiping his sweaty brow with a handkerchief. Dendron looked sharp and alert, while Epsilon looked scared and out of place.

Severus addressed the assembly.

"I am going to expose the person who tried to kill the Emperor by putting a poisonous cobra in his bed. This same person ordered Pudens to participate in the assassination plot and in the end to kill himself. This person is an agent of the *spasaka*, the Eye of the Great King, the Persian secret service. This person is in this courtroom, in the corona, facing me, as I am facing him. You know who you are, of course, but rest assured that I now know who you are as well. And I will tell you how I know.

"When it was learned by the *curiosi* that the *spasaka* had set in motion a plot to assassinate our Emperors, Lucius Verus and Marcus Aurelius, it was already too late for Lucius Verus. He was dead. Whether he died naturally from a stroke or whether the stroke was induced by poison or some other murderous method, we will never know. However, I had to make an assumption that anyone who was a member of the entourages of both Emperors became a person of interest, even a suspect, because it was a *sine qua non* for the assassin to get physically close to his victim. And although at first we didn't know whether the information we had about an assassin was true or not, that all changed with the recent attempt to assassinate Marcus Aurelius.

"You all know that an Egyptian cobra was put in the Emperor's bed in the Imperial villa at Lanuvium. By luck, the Emperor was called back to Rome shortly before he was to take his usual afternoon nap in the bed where a cobra was waiting for him under the blankets. The cobra was later found by a cleaning slave and killed by Lothar."

Severus looked at the Praetorian who returned a self-satisfied smile.

"Where did that cobra come from?" continued the judge. "We know it was bought, two snakes were bought, from the Marsic cult of snake charmers at Lake Fucinus. They were purchased by Obesus, the aide to the *munerarius*, ostensibly for the purpose of using them in the execution of criminals during the next Games at the Flavian amphitheater. His slave Nush had some experience in handling snakes, he told me, from when he was a boy in Persia. Nush selected the snakes from the Marsic cult and took them back to Rome in wicker baskets.

"In Rome one of the snakes was almost immediately turned over by Obesus to Publius Pudens, who with the help of Nush as the snake's handler, took it away with him. A few days later, Pudens organized a trip to the Imperial villa at Lanuvium, supposedly to visit his sister Plautilla who was there as a member of Aurelius' entourage. Actually, Pudens went there to take part in the assassination of the Emperor. He brought the Egyptian cobra with him in a wicker basket strapped to the top of the second of two *carpenta* carrying his luggage, litter and slaves.

"Why did Pudens do this? Why was he a traitor to Rome, an agent for Persia? I am told he was an ardent follower of the Persian cult of Mithra, the result of experiencing the bitterness of life and the ineffectiveness of the Roman and Greek gods. He had become an unhappy, hateful person. He turned against his own country and tried to find salvation in a foreign cult. It's not such an unfamiliar outcome; there are plenty of examples of Romans becoming followers of foreign cults, and plenty of examples of civil strife. More than a few Emperors have been assassinated by Romans, as we all know.

"But as it turned out, Pudens was ordered by a Lion in the Mithra cult, a member of the *spasaka*, to aid in the plot to assassinate our Emperors. He accepted that role. As a Mithraic Soldier, he became a tool of the Persian assassin.

"You may ask where I get this information about Pudens and why I should believe it? Mostly it comes from his freedman and secretary Dendron, who says Pudens told him these things while he was preparing to commit suicide. A last confession, so to speak, a catharsis. Now Dendron admits that he killed Pudens by cutting his throat, but alleges that it was at Pudens' own request. Like aiding a suicide to fall on his sword. But is that what really happened? Did Dendron help Pudens commit suicide? Or did he murder him?"

Severus looked at his court clerk who promptly handed him a scroll. "The answer is given by Pudens himself, in his will, signed, sealed and put in the care of his Vestal sister. There is no doubt about the will's authenticity. It is in his own writing, as I have determined. How does the will resolve the question, suicide or murder? Here is the will. I have already opened Pudens' intact seal. It says,"

> "I give a bequest of 100 gold aurei to
> my freedman and secretary Dendron
> for helping me to commit suicide in the
> way I want to die. Quickly. I asked him
> to cut my throat. I also instructed him
> to tell others that I died by cutting my

wrists and bleeding to death in a warm bath."

Severus let the scroll furl back up and looked at Dendron. "Though I previously doubted Dendron and thought he probably murdered Pudens, I now think differently. Pudens' will is the proof.

"Now I want to return to what Pudens did to carry out the instructions of his Persian master. We know he brought the Egyptian cobra to Lanuvium in a wicker basket on top of one of the coaches. But Pudens couldn't have personally put the snake in the Emperor's bed because he had left Lanuvium for Rome the day before. So obviously someone else, someone at the villa, put the snake in the Emperor's bed. Who? From a joke Pudens once made to Dendron when he was preparing his suicide, it was a lion who put the snake to bed. The lion is the Persian assassin. But who is the lion?"

"To answer that question, I want to jump ahead for the moment and make a connection with what occurred when Pudens learned he would be tried for treason in my court.

"When I sent him a 5-day notice of trial, the next day in the afternoon he left his *domus* by himself and went somewhere, we don't know where, and evidently discussed the situation with his superior in the Mithra cult. We know this because that evening he received a message on a wax tablet."

Severus took the tablet from a fold of his toga, opened it and read. "'Lion to Soldier. Kill yourself.' Soldier was Pudens' rank in the Mithra cult. Lion is a rank superior to Soldier. Upon receiving this message,

Pudens began to prepare for his own suicide, making out his will and arranging for Dendron to help him kill himself.

"What is most revealing about this scenario is that Pudens' superior, the Lion, the Mithra cult member, the person who put the snake in the Emperor's bed, the *spasaka* agent, must have been in Rome. That was because one afternoon and evening is not time enough to get a message and reply between Rome and Lanuvium, let alone allow time for any discussion of what was to happen. Even the fastest horse relay system of the *cursus publicus* couldn't do it in that time. Consequently, the five suspects who I had confined to the Imperial villa and who were still there on the day Pudens contacted his Lion, could not have been that Lion. Therefore, I do not believe any of you in the first row were the accomplices of Pudens in the treason plot. You are therefore all exonerated. So please step out of the courtroom and wait outside. I may call you back for testimony if necessary."

Severus motioned to them to get up and exit the courtroom. The five could hardly believe what they were hearing. The doctor glared at Severus as if to say 'I told you so', while Jangi and Eclectus looked relieved. Plautilla took it as a matter of course. Lothar just followed her out.

Severus turned his attention to the four remaining people in the corona, Obesus, Nush, Dendron and Epsilon.

"There is another conclusion to be drawn from Pudens' excursion to meet the Lion that afternoon and the message to kill himself that arrived at his house that evening. And that conclusion is that the Lion, the *spasaka* agent, was not someone who was living in Pudens' *domus*. If he were, there would have been no need to go out of the house to talk to him and no message would have come to the house in return. So Dendron and Epsilon, you are exonerated. You may step outside, but wait, because I may call you back in for evidence."

He motioned to them to leave. That left Obesus and Nush in the corona. "Obesus, you were not on the expedition to Lanuvium, so you could not be the lion who put the snake to bed. You can leave."

Obesus darted out of the courtroom, once again "as fast as cooking asparagus".

"That leaves you, Nush. You were at Lanuvium with Pudens and you were in Rome, at the Castra Praetoria, the afternoon that Pudens sought out the Lion."

"There is a mistake you are making. I left Lanuvium with Pudens when he left for Rome, the day before the snake was put in the Emperor's bed, according to your timetable. If Pudens couldn't have done it because he wasn't there, neither could I."

"Yes, that would exclude you *if* you weren't there. But while you said you left the villa in the second *carpentum* with the slaves, Epsilon told me the other day that you were in the first coach with Pudens and Dendron. So where were you really? Were you actually in any of the coaches? Tell me now, which *carpentum* were you in? The first with Pudens and Dendron or the second with the slaves?"

"I don't really remember."

Severus turned to one of the lictors. "Bring back Dendron." The lictor went out and returned with Dendron.

"Dendron," said Severus to him, "on the return journey from Lanuvium to Rome which *carpentum* were you in?

"The first, with Pudens. Just like the way we came"

"Where was Nush?"

"I thought he was in the second *carpentum*, just like the way we came."

"Did you see him in the second coach?"

"No, not really. He did come over to our coach to say something to Pudens before we headed out, but then he went away. I assumed he entered the second coach. But I didn't actually see him do it."

"You may leave." Severus told the lictor. "Now bring in Epsilon."

The lictor returned with the slave.

"Epsilon, when you returned to Rome from Lanuvium, was Nush in your coach? You told me the other day he was in the first *carpentum*."

"He wasn't in the second coach, that I know. I saw him at one point talking to our master Pudens in the first *carpentum*, so I assumed he was traveling with him. But I didn't actually see him in that coach."

"You may leave." Severus turned back to Nush. "So you weren't in either coach. That means you re- mained at the villa."

"Nonsense. And even if I were at the villa how could I have contrived to put the snake in the Emperor's bed? I would have been seen as a stranger wandering in the corridors of the villa, wouldn't I? I couldn't have gotten anywhere near the bedroom. I wouldn't even know where it was. And how could I even bring a snake in?"

"You would know all about the Emperor's bedroom and where it was because Pudens deliberately took a tour of the villa and bribed the *cubicularius* to allow him to enter the bedroom. He saw the set up and told you all about it. As to how it was you weren't noticed, I have a theory that I believe is most probably what happened. Who gets to wander about the corridors of the villa with wicker baskets without question? Cleaning slaves that's who. Women dressed in gray tunics with gray kerchiefs on their heads. You could easily have put on clothes like that. You have a certain feminine gait, as everyone has noticed. So you could have easily impersonated a cleaning woman, taken the snake in the wicker basket into the bedroom and released it under the covers. After all, who else would know how to handle a poisonous viper? Then you would simply have left the villa. Probably Pudens had arranged for a coach to pick you up somewhere a short distance from the villa and take you back to Rome. I will undertake to locate that coach, if you deny that's what happened.

"And there will also be another proof. When Pudens left his house to meet the Lion that afternoon, he met you didn't he? He must have gone to the Castra Praetoria where you were and asked to see his former slave. The timing fits too. Pudens was out all that afternoon. It takes about an hour to walk from his house on the Aventine Hill to the Castra Praetoria and an hour back. Leave an hour or so for his meeting with the Lion and his afternoon is accounted for. When he reached the Castra Praetoria, Nush, someone must have brought you out to meet him or let him in to see you. Remember he was dressed as a member of the Senatorial Order, in a toga with the broad stripe on his tunic visible. That's how he could readily get to you. Someone, some guard, some slave will remember the incident. I will find those people if you deny it. So tell me, Nush, isn't that what happened?"

Nush closed his eyes and thought. Everyone was silent. They waited. It seemed a long time. After at least a quarter of an hour, Vulso and Straton looked at the judge questioningly, as if asking him to prompt an answer. But Severus shook his head 'no' and remained patiently waiting. Eventually Nush opened his eyes and looked at his questioners, one after the other. Then his gaze settled on Judge Severus. He took a deep breath and spoke forthrightly and proudly.

"Judge Severus, I was grateful to you for freeing me from what you thought was a disastrous slave situation that I said I was in. Of course, my stories of being raped by Pudens were nonsense. I controlled him, not the other way around. I am a Lion, he a mere Soldier. But while I admire your *humanitas*, as you Romans call it, I also bathe in the warm waters of my own cleverness at outwitting you. I am not a slave. I was not abused by anyone. But I convinced you otherwise."

Severus nodded in silent agreement.

"Now, Judge Severus, I have to salute you again for figuring out what happened. Yes, it happened exactly as you describe it. I remained at the villa when

Pudens and the others left. I impersonated a woman cleaning slave and knew where to put the cobra because Pudens had been inside the bedroom and told me about it. Then I left the villa, as you said, and was picked up by a *carpentum* that Pudens arranged to meet me on the road to Rome."

Severus took a deep breath and relaxed in his magistrate's chair. Brennus and the four *curiosi* agents standing in the back converged on Nush and picked him up, put handcuffs on him, and rapidly took him away.

"Now," said Severus, smiling broadly, "we can all go to our *insula* on the Caelian Hill and celebrate. The Persian assassin has been caught."

EPILOGUE

MARCUS FLAVIUS SEVERUS: TO HIMSELF

One day a few months later, I was in Rome to be a witness in a law suit between the *advocatus fisci*, the lawyer for the Treasury, as plaintiff, and Plautilla, Pudens' sister as defendant. The issue is who gets Pudens' money and property, the Treasury or his sister, as his heir.

The Treasury claims that Pudens committed suicide while charged with treason and treason has as one of its penalties forfeiture of all property to the State. The Treasury relies on a Rescript of the Emperor Antoninus Pius ruling that suicide before conviction in treason cases does not avoid forfeiture.

The position of Plautilla, however, is that Pudens was murdered. In that case, there could be no forfeiture and she would inherit his property as his heir.

Both sides agreed that Dendron cut Pudens' throat at his request. But was that a suicide or a murder? An esoteric legal point, perhaps, but a lot of money is riding on the outcome. After all, a member of the Senatorial Order, like Pudens, has to have at least a million sesterces to maintain that rank in society.

As a sidelight, whatever the result, Dendron cannot get the 100 gold *aurei* that Pudens left him in his will. That's because if it was a suicide, the Treasury gets the money. If it was a murder, in Roman law the murderer cannot profit from his crime.

The result? As far as I know, the case is still dragging through the courts and could drag on for years, as often happens. Eventually it may have to be decided by the Emperor in his court. Or it may be settled. Who knows?

While I was in Rome, though, my thoughts turned to Nush, wondering what had happened to him. It is ironic for me to admit this, even to myself, but I'm sorry the Persian assassin turned out to be Nush. He had a way about him, an ingratiating manner perhaps, but one which made you like him, almost trust him. I suppose that's what made him a good agent of the *spasaka*. That's what allowed him to pass as a slave, while actually he was a Lion.

After the *curiosi* took Nush out of my courtroom, no one would ever hear about him again. No one would ever know what happened to him. The *curiosi* is a secret agency, becoming an empire within an empire, and secrecy is one of its hallmarks. Getting information from them is impossible, like trying "to milk a male goat,"as the saying goes.

However, during an off-day in the trial over Pudens' property, on an impulse I sent a message to

Brennus at *curiosi* headquarters, asking him to come see me. He did, and I then asked him what happened to Nush.

He said the *curiosi* never tells about such things, unless it serves their purpose.

I asked him to conclude that it would serve their purpose to tell me.

He didn't make a fuss about it. He just shrugged and said "all right." He then told me, "we squeezed all we could out of him. He told us everything he knew about the *spasaka*'s internal and external workings, the names of *spasaka* agents inside Persia and in our Empire. Some information he gave up rapidly, some only under torture. And he told us how the *spasaka* worked, who their leaders were, everything we've always wanted to know.

"But, and this is a large but, we don't really know what is true and what is false about what Nush told us, even under torture. He may have given us the names of Mithra cult personnel in Rome who were actually loyal Romans. How could we corroborate that they are disloyal except under torture, and what kind of corroboration is that? Everything Nush told us might have been a lie. Probably some of it is true, but what is and what isn't, we just don't know. Nush was very clever, very well trained, and completely opaque. I was always under the impression that while we thought we were squeezing information out of him, he was actually feeding us false information. I was under the distinct impression he was outwitting us.

"We finally executed him. But he was still defiant, even then. At the end, he said his name Nush was short for the Persian word *anausha*, meaning immortal. He said that like the 10,000 Persian Immortals, the personal guard and standing army of the old Persian *Shahanshah*, when one Immortal died or fell out, another would immediately replace him. That way there were always 10,000 Immortals in existence. The formation was immortal. It was like that with the *spasaka*, he warned us. We could kill him, but it would make no difference. There would be another just like him as a replacement."

"An ominous thought," I commented.

"Yes, an ominous thought," he agreed. "But here's something curious," he added. "Originally we were going to execute him slowly and painfully, by crucifixion. Doesn't Herodotus tell us that crucifixion was invented by the Persians? So what could be more fitting. But in the end, despite the fact that he was our enemy, we all came to like him. His torturers, his interrogators, we all admired him. And so we decided to execute him in the quickest, most painless and honorable way. We beheaded him."

I told all this to my wife later that night, asking what was my part in all this. I'm not going to stop the conflict between Rome and Iran. Greece and Rome have been fighting wars with Persia and Parthia on and off since Darius was defeated by the Athenians at Marathon, and that was more than 650 years ago. There have been many wars in the past, and I suppose there will be many more in the future. There have been spies and assassins in the past, there are now, and there will be more in the future. What did I have to do with any of this?

She said that I had likely saved the life of the Emperor, of my friend. What more did I want?

Her terse reply summed it up. There was nothing more I wanted. The Fates had dragged me in. They had their way with me. Now I just wanted to retire from it all.

Then let's do that, she said. I want to write my book on Aspasia. Maybe you should write a book too.

Maybe I should, I thought. Maybe I should.

HISTORICAL NOTE

Information about Roman spies, intelligence activities, fire signaling, the *curiosi* and the Persian 'Eye of the King', the *spasaka*. etc. is primarily from Francis Dvornik, *Origins of Intelligence Services*, (Rutgers U. Press, 1974); Rose Mary Sheldon, *Intelligence Activities in Ancient Rome: Trust in the gods, but Verify.* (Frank Cass, 2005); N.J.E.Austin & N.B.Rankov, *Exploratio: Military and Political Intelligence in the Roman World* (Routledge, 1995); Sinnigen, William G., The Roman Secret Service, The Classical Journal, vol. 57. No. 2 (Nov. 1961) pp. 65-72; Lendering, Jona, Eye of the King, http://www.livius.org/es=ez/eyes/eyes.html.

No one really knows the extent of the activities of ancient intelligence activities in the ancient world, but we know they existed. The 'Eyes and Ears of the king' were not only part of the Persian government but were part of the ancient Egyptian state as well. Except for a discussion of some methods of Chinese spies in Sun Tzu, *The Art of War*, secret services did not reveal what they did, or if they did, it has not survived. But from what we know about empires and their internal security and foreign intelligence measures, we can well believe that they were not only secret, but extensive, and inclined to grow their power. Indeed, the Roman secret service, first as the *frumentarii*, colloquially the *curiosi*, then in the reconstituted form of *agentes in rebus*, i.e. general agents, actually outlived the fall of the Roman Empire, still existing as a bureaucratic entity after the last Roman Emperor in the west was gone.

The Augustan histories of Lucius Verus and Marcus Aurelius mention that the doctor who bled Lucius Verus when he had his stroke was named Posidippus and a certain Eclectus was a *cubicularius* for Verus and then taken on by Marcus Aurelius. Moreover, the accusations against the doctor for killing Verus by incompetently or purposely bleeding him were leveled against him at the time. SHA *Marcus*, XV. 5-6; *Verus*, IX. 5-6. Though we know the names of Posidippus and Eclectus, no one knows their character and so I apologize to them if I got it wrong. However, I've used the names of Posidippus and Eclectus for a certain historical verisimilitude. The other suspects, Jangi, Plautilla and Lothar are invented. The Urban Prefect Lucius Sergius Paullus and the Consul P. Coellius Apollonaris were the actual Prefect and Consul at the time the story is set.

As for the antics of Commodus as a child, his buffoonery and expertise in whistling are reported in the Augustan Histories at SHA *Commodus*, I.8.

The method of murdering by pricking a victim with a poisoned needle is mentioned twice by Dio

Cassius. LXVII.11.6; LXXIII. 14.4. This method is still in use 2,000 years later, as North Koreans reportedly assassinated the brother of Kim Jong-un at an airport with a poisoned needle in 2017.

Details about Mithraism, its doctrines, rituals and practices come from, *inter alia*, Robert Turcan, *Cults of the Roman Empire* (Blackwell, 1996) pp,195-247; Manfred Clauss, *The Roman Cult of Mithras: The God and his Mysteries*, (Routledge, 2001); Roger Beck, *The Religion of the Mithras Cult in the Roman Empire* (Oxford U. Press 2006).

Galen's medical ideas on bleeding, the thinning diet, etc. come from *Galen: Selected Works*, translated P.N.Singer (Oxford 1997); Mark Grant, *Galen on Food and Diet* (Routledge 2001); Also, Susan P. Mattern, *The Prince of Medicine: Galen in the Roman Empire* (Oxford U. Press 2013).

The fresco on the cover is from the wall of a Roman bedroom at Boscoreale, near Pompeii. This bedroom has been recreated at the Metropolitan Museum of Art in New York City.

The map of the vicinity of Rome on page xvi is from Everyman's Library, *Atlas of Ancient and Classical Geography,* (London, New York 1950).

Once again, I would like to thank Ruth Chevion for her careful and insightful editing, her excellent suggestions and useful discussions about the book, and especially for her loving care, support and encouragement over many years.

Made in the USA
Middletown, DE
16 September 2022

10631021R00146